# FORGING CHAOS

## FORGING
## BOOK 3

## LAINEY DAVIS

Editing by Becky with Bookcase Media

# ABOUT THE BOOK

**Sometimes, you have to lose everything to win what matters most.**

I had it all–speed, skill, and a one-way ticket to the pros. But one bad hit shattered my career and left me with a busted leg, a bruised ego, and no clue what comes next.

Enter Thora, my no-nonsense research partner who's too smart, too fierce, and too beautiful for a washed-up guy like me. She's got a sharp mind, big dreams, and zero patience for my pity party. Plus, she sees straight through my game face to all the broken parts of me, and instead of running away, she challenges me to do better.

But just when I'm starting to believe I could have a second chance–with life and with her–she drops a bombshell: she's leaving. Heading halfway across the world to chase her own dreams.

I've lost one future already, but there's no way I'll lose this one, too. Thora's heart is the only prize that matters, and I am ready to go all in.

# CHAPTER 1
# ODIN

I WAKE UP IN A HAZE, my vision blurry and unfocused. Not sure why, but there are some harsh fluorescent lights above me. Something smells like chemicals—antiseptic.

Panic rises in my chest as I try to piece together what happened. I attempt to sit up, but a sharp, searing pain shoots through my ankle, forcing me back down with a groan.

Last thing I knew, I was flying down the football field, defense bouncing off me like hailstones—until one of them didn't, and I went down like I'd been struck by lightning.

The memory hits me like a freight train - the game, the tackle, the sickening pop as I went down.

I was hoping it was a dream.

Instead, it is a nightmare.

I know where I am.

Reality crashes down like thunder: I'm in a hospital bed.

Did I at least score the touchdown?

The thought flits past, and I almost laugh at how ridiculous it seems now. Here I am, laid up in a hospital bed, and I'm worried about whether I got the ball over the line in a stupid spring scrimmage that doesn't mean anything. But that's who I am - or who I was. Odin Stag, star running back.

The guy whose entire future hinged on his ability to dodge tackles and sprint down a field.

I just yeeted my Achilles, and I know what that means.

So, what am I now? A patient. A statistic. Another athlete whose dreams just fizzled out like a passing storm.

I'm pulled from my spiral of self-pity by the sound of the door opening. My mom walks in, her eyes red-rimmed. Dad's right behind her, his usual happy expression cracking around the edges. I can see the worry etched into the lines of his face, the fear he's trying so hard to hide.

"Hey, kiddo," Dad says, his voice gruff with emotion. "How're you feeling?"

I paste on my best grin, determined not to let them see how scared I really am. "Like I just went ten rounds with a freight train," I quip. "But you should see the other guy."

Usually, this sort of thing has Dad roaring, coming back with bad puns. Today, he just nods. Mom lets out a watery chuckle, perching on the edge of my bed. She married a hockey player. Ty Stag—Pittsburgh legend. None of this should be new to her, but I guess it's different when it's your kid laid up like this.

Her hand finds mine, squeezing gently. "Oh, sweetie," she murmurs. "We were so worried."

Before I can respond, the door swings open again, and a doctor strides in, all business. He knows my dad, because of course he does, and they shoot the shit until the doc seems to remember I'm here. He launches into an explanation of my injury, throwing around terms like "complete rupture" and "surgical intervention." I try to follow along, but my mind keeps catching on to phrases like "extended recovery time" and "physical therapy."

What does this mean for my future? For the draft next year? For everything I've worked so hard to achieve?

My parents pepper the doctor with questions I can't bring myself to ask. How long until I can walk? Run? Play again?

Each answer feels like another nail in the coffin of my dreams. As the doctor leaves, an uncomfortable silence settles over the room. Things must really be bad if Dad isn't making a dumb joke about deodorant or trying to grab Mom's butt.

"Well," Dad says finally, forcing a smile, "at least this gives you some time to focus on class, right? Might even boost that GPA of yours."

I know he's trying to help, to find some positive in all this, but it just makes me feel worse. Their presence feels suffocating right now. I'm torn between wanting their comfort and needing space to process this on my own.

I'm surprised my entire extended family isn't here right now. The Stag family bench is deep, with three uncles, three aunts, and seven cousins usually up in my business. But I remember that they *were* all here before the surgery, and Dad sent them home when I went under the knife. I don't want to see the entire extended crew right now. I don't want to see anyone.

First, I need to figure out who I am now.

My drug-addled mind repeats a bunch of thoughts. I'm not going to be a professional athlete. I might not even be able to be an Uber driver. And I know damn well my family will want me to look on some bright side or keep my spirits high or whatever rainbow bullshit.

Right now, I need to focus on the realities of what's going on with my body: agony, yes, but also…deterioration. A torn Achilles is very much an Achilles heel. A career-ending injury. That's just math.

I've spent my entire life planning a professional sports career. I was raised by an Olympic rowing mother and a professional hockey player father, and all my brothers are gearing up to follow in Dad's footsteps. Where does that leave me? Even after I physically recover from this nightmare, I won't be the same person I was before.

I was my Norse god namesake … wielding lightning or

some shit. Now, I'm a has-been in an entire family of superstars.

"Odin?" Mom places her hand on my arm, and I meet her eye.

I clear my throat and ask her to take me to the bathroom to have something to do. Mom presses her lips into a line. "Honey, you're not supposed to get out of bed yet…"

I squint and look over my left shoulder at a catheter bag full of piss. I laugh. I can't even control my bladder right now. I am totally, utterly at the mercy of these machines. Yet, the reality of it is that I haven't been controlling anything for years. I eat what Coach tells me to. I lift what another coach tells me to lift. I follow the rigid path toward the pros because that's my legacy.

That's the plan.

But not anymore.

I sigh and reach for the clicker the nurse told me about with my morphine drip. I click until the monitors start to beep, and I fall asleep listening to my parents in manic planning mode with a zillion different specialists huddled around my bed.

# CHAPTER 2
# THORA

RATIONALLY, I know I didn't curse anyone. It's just plain lousy timing that Odin Stag happened to get hurt moments after I complained about having to work with him on my final project for a class I absolutely need to ace.

People complain about group projects all the time. Just small talk. How was I supposed to know he'd go down like a dump truck full of gravel the second I finished my rant about him being a shitty research partner.

It's not that I think he's not smart. I don't trust anyone but my best friend Fern.

Anyway, just in case the universe is testing me, I'm making Odin cookies. At home in my parents' kitchen with the window open and a fan blowing to keep the plume of my father's cigarette smoke away from the baked goods.

I really don't bake. But how hard can it be to follow the instructions on a bag of chocolate chips? I'm pretty pleased when the first pan I pull from the oven looks exactly like the photo on the bag, like actual, regular cookies. I smile, scraping them from the pan onto a towel I set on the table. We don't have any foil, and we certainly don't have the cooling racks the instructions recommended. Hell, we only have one cookie sheet, and it looks like it's been in the house for five decades.

My dad must have caught a whiff of the cookie's success because he hollers, "Bring me a few of those, will you?"

I grind my teeth. Nothing is preventing him from getting up from the couch himself. It's one thing when he asks me to bring him a drink on my way past. I'm not working today. I'm not waiting on people. Plus, these are spoken for.

I ignore him and get to work scooping balls of dough onto the pan for the second batch, thinking about Fern's offer to accompany me to Odin's apartment to deliver the cookies. She's dating his cousin, who also lives there. I encouraged her to make a move on Wyatt, and that seems to have worked out great. Fern assures me nobody has mentioned a single thing about me having cursed Odin into a significant injury.

It's self-centered of me to even imagine I caused this. I'm well aware. I lick a wayward hunk of dough from the outside of my hand before I slide the pan into the oven. I'm well on my way toward a peace offering I plan to combine with a reasonable insistence that I take care of the entire project for our shared class. If Odin is hurt, he'll have much to deal with recovering. That's just facts.

"You hear me?" Dad's voice startles me. He stands at the entrance to the kitchen, leaning against the wall with his arms crossed. "I asked you to bring me one of those."

I swallow back the urge to point out he *demanded* several of the cookies. Instead, I smile and explain, "These are a gift for a friend, Dad. He's sick."

He steps toward the stove. "You can make a few extra for your own family. If he's sick, he can't eat all that."

I place my body between my father and the cookies. "They're not for you." My voice is sharp, harsher than I ever speak to my parents, even though they provide absolutely nothing for me at this point in my life. My scholarship covers rent for me to live here, more than my fair share of the groceries. I've helped pay my way in the world since I was tall enough to work under the table at all the shitty restaurants my parents bounced between. I'm leaving here in a few months, just as long as I maintain my perfect grade point average and meet the expectations of my graduate school fellowship.

Dad's lip curls up angrily. "Think you're better than us now? Cookies for your fancy school friends? Is that it?"

I shake my head. "That's not it at all. These cookies are a gift. For someone in pain."

My father looks at me like I'm the enemy and turns on his heel, heading back to the living room, muttering about how his own kid won't cut him a break.

I realize there's no way the entire batch of cookies will fit in the empty nut container I brought home from the bar. After I clean up the kitchen, I glance at the overflow, about eight beautiful cookies. I fight an impulse to cram them in my mouth or shove them in the garbage. Instead, I pile them on a plate, leave them on the table, and walk out the back door with my get-well gift for Odin.

# CHAPTER 3
## ODIN

BY MORNING, I'm exhausted from nurses entering my room every five minutes overnight. They're gradually pulling tubes out of my body, which is great, but I would pay any amount of money right now for an hour of uninterrupted sleep.

I pay casual attention as the morning nurse reviews plans with me. Something about benchmarks to put weight on my foot and later to drive. I'm getting a knee roller and fancy physical therapy courtesy of the university football team, but I'm entirely dependent on others to get me to and from the facility. Great.

They pulled the tube out of my junk so at least I could pee on my own...under supervision and with several orderlies holding me upright. What a hero I am. If only the jersey chasers could see me now.

The nurse tells me to prepare for discharge around lunchtime and leaves me in peace, but the door to my room bursts open again immediately.

This time, it's a girl I vaguely recognize from one of my classes. She's with my roommate Stellan, who looms behind her, tugging at his shirt collar.

What the hell?

Thora, I think her name is. She's tiny and loud in class, and I think I'm supposed to work with her on a project. She's clutching a metal container to her chest, looking flustered and out of breath.

"Odin!" she exclaims and rushes to my bedside like we've known each other for years. "I brought you cookies."

Stellan leans on the wall, clearly out of breath from trying to keep up with this pint-sized, treat-yielding woman. I'm about to ask what the hell she's doing here when she barrels on, "I feel responsible for this." She waves a hand around at my leg, which is engulfed in my brand-new plastic boot. "I was bitching about working with you, and there you were on the television. And then all this happened. Not that I think I control evil demons or something. I'm not the real Thora."

I stare at her. "Am I high? Are you here right now?"

Stellan waves. "She showed up at the apartment. I offered to bring her in. She has cookies." He points at the tin, and she nods.

"I am sorry to interrupt while you're sick. Are you sick? Injured. It's just that I wanted to let you know…about our class project. It's due soon, and with you being…well, here, I wasn't sure how we were going to finish it, and I need this grade to maintain my scholarship, and-"

I cut her off, overwhelmed. "Seriously? I'm lying here in a robotic cast with my career in shambles, and you're worried about a class project?"

Thora's face falls, and I see the moment she realizes how she's come across. "I- I'm sorry," she stammers. "I didn't mean…Of course, your health is the most important thing. I just… I cannot get a bad grade on this assignment. I have a fellowship lined up for grad school, and I can't lose it. I was wondering if you wanted me to go ahead and do the whole project. And I made you cookies."

Something in her voice, in the desperate look in her eyes,

makes me pause. She waves the metal tin at me, and I reach for it. For the first time, I look at Thora—not just as the bossy, intense girl from class but as a person with dreams and fears. Plus, I know something about losing a shot at a big dream.

"Grad school, huh?" I say, my tone softer now. "What are you going to study?"

I fumble with the cookie tin lid as Stellan scratches his neck.

Thora reaches for the container and opens it for me, handing me a cookie. I feel a little zing as our fingers touch, but it's probably because I'm high on painkillers. Or something.

She tells me she won an award and is going to study international policy in England. I can't keep up. The meds are kicking in big time, and I'm groggy and struggling to chew the cookie. When I open my eyes again, I see Thora holding the foam cup of water near my face, tapping my cheek with the straw.

Is she taking charge of this situation? I don't hate it.

I sip and meet her eye, not sure what I see there, which tracks, because I'm not sure of anything right now.

I swallow the water and say, "Thank you." She nods and sets the cup back on the table. I try to move the container of cookies, but my arms aren't paying attention to my brain right now.

I arch a brow. Or maybe I squint. I'm not sure, but Thora shifts her weight uncomfortably. Stellan sighs and walks over to the bed, placing his palm on my head like he's some sort of priest offering a blessing. "Hey, man," he grunts. "Sucks about your foot."

I nod. At least, I think I do. He shakes his head and reaches for a cookie, but I have just enough concentration left to swat his arm out of the way. "Those are mine," I growl.

Thora presses her lips together. "Okay, well, I wrote my

cell on the cookie container. I don't need it back, by the way. I just wanted you to be able to contact me. About class."

Stellan sets a hand on her shoulder, and something unpleasant flicks through my chest. What's his deal with Thora? He says, "I'll take you back to the apartment."

She shakes her head. "No, thanks. Fern and Wyatt are going to be making up for lost time." She checks her watch. "I have a shift soon. I can walk."

Stellan frowns at her and glances at me. I try to frown at him. Something is off about this. I wish my head were working. He groans and says, "I'll drop you at the bar, okay? And I won't touch any more of his cookies." My cousin tosses a grin at me and then walks out of the room, squeezing my good leg on his way out the door. Thora follows, looking uneasy. I can't get a read on her.

But then, I can't get a read on anything right now. Except I'm pretty sure she plowed in here to tell me she's going to do our whole project without me, and that stings more than my incision. I am literally not in control of any part of my life, from my digestion to my rehab schedule.

Maybe I can handle a group project.

"Don't count on doing the paper alone," I bark.

She turns to face me from the hall, brow furrowed. "Sorry, what?"

"It's a team grade," I tell her, tapping my fingers on the metal container that looks like it used to contain multiple pounds of shelled and salted peanuts. "We're a team. We'll do it together."

Stellan blinks at me, and Thora taps her foot on the floor. "Maybe just call me when you're home," she says. I can tell she thinks I'll forget this conversation. She and Stellan leave, and I stare at the ceiling, waiting for discharge. I give up and fall asleep, thinking about Thora's pouty lips as she offered me water.

# CHAPTER 4
## THORA

I SLIP INTO FUEL UP, the trendy bar where I work too many hours, my mind a whirlwind. The familiar scent of stale beer and greasy bar food hits me, but it does nothing to calm my nerves after seeing Odin so messed up. My hands shake as I tie my apron, and I nearly drop a glass while setting up the bar.

"Real smooth, Thora," I mutter to myself. "First, you act like a weird robot in front of the injured hottie, and now you can't even handle basic bartending tasks. A stellar day all around."

As I start serving the early crowd, my mind keeps replaying the scene at the hospital. Odin's shocked face when I burst in, babbling about our project like some kind of sociopathic academic drone. God, there I was, this crazy-eyed loudmouth, more concerned about a class assignment than Odin's injury.

A customer snaps his fingers at me, jarring me back to reality. "Hey, sweetheart, you gonna stand there all day, or can I get another beer?"

I plaster on my best fake smile. "Coming right up, sir. And

hey, maybe we could work on using our words instead of treating me like a dog? Just a thought."

As I pour his beer–extra foam because fuck him–I can't help but draw parallels between this interaction and my behavior at the hospital. Was I any better than this entitled jerk demanding Odin's attention when he was clearly in pain? Some Rhodes Scholar I am. I can't even manage basic human empathy. Although … I didn't infantilize Odin with a chauvinistic pet name, so at least there's that.

The bar door swings open, and in walks Fern, practically floating in a post-sex haze. I'm happy she had a reunion with her hottie. Odin's cousin, I remember. Family.

Fern's hair is mussed, and a small blue bruise is peeking out from under her collar. I raise an eyebrow as she approaches.

"You and Wyatt made nice, I take it?"

Fern grins, unabashed. "Oh, hush. You were the one who turned me into this person. What is it you always say? Stick a peen in it and forget for a while?"

Her words sting more than they should. "Yeah, well, some of us have more pressing concerns than getting our rocks off."

Fern's smile falters. "Okay, spill. What happened at the hospital? And don't say 'nothing.' I know your 'I fucked up' face, and you're wearing it hard right now."

I sigh, glancing around to make sure no customers need me before leaning in. "I may have royally screwed up with Odin today."

"How? Didn't you give him the cookies? Men love cookies."

I groan, recounting my disastrous hospital visit. With each word, Fern's eyes grow wider. When I finish, she lets out a low whistle.

"Wow. That's...something."

"I know. Who does that? Who bursts into a hospital room

and immediately starts talking about a class project? I'm a monster, Fern. A grade-obsessed, compassionless monster."

Fern reaches across the bar, grabbing my hand. "Hey, stop that. You're not a monster. You're just...intensely focused. And under a shit-ton of pressure."

I snort. "Yeah, because that makes it so much better. God, what if they revoke my fellowship? 'Sorry, Ms. Janssen, we've decided you lack the basic human decency required to represent our institution.'"

"Thora, breathe. They're not going to revoke your fellowship over one awkward interaction. And let's be real, you've got so much riding on this project. It's not unreasonable to be worried about it."

I nod, knowing she has a point. But the guilt still gnaws at me. "I just...I should have been better, you know? He's lying there with his life in shambles, and all I could think about was my stupid GPA. A rational person would have just sent the cookies with his cousin. And a note."

The bar starts to fill up, and I throw myself into work, grateful for the distraction. But even as I mix drinks and fake laugh at terrible jokes, my mind keeps drifting back to Odin. To the way his blue eyes had widened in surprise when I burst in, to the hurt that had flashed across his face at my callousness.

During a lull, I can't help but check my phone. No messages. Not that I expected any, but still. My finger hovers over Odin's contact info that Stellan gave me when we left the hospital. He was weird about it, too, like I'm interested in Odin for sexy times and not just a means to a four-point-oh.

Should I text Odin? Apologize? But what would I even say? 'Sorry I acted like a robot with no feelings. Hope your catastrophic injury isn't too inconvenient for my academic goals.'

Fuck that. I did offer to do the whole project so it could be one less thing he worries about. Is academic integrity important to him? I don't know which way is up at the moment.

So, instead, I respond to a text from my mom, firmly telling her that no, I will not stop for cigarettes for Dad on my way home. I wish this happened rarely enough that I was shocked about the request, but I am not.

As the night winds down, Fern finishes chatting with the staff and prepares to leave. She fixes me with a stern look. "Promise me you'll be kind to yourself, okay? You're allowed to have conflicting feelings. You're allowed to worry about your future and still care about others."

I roll my eyes, but I can feel a small smile tugging at my lips. "Yes, Mom. I promise to practice positive self-talk and all that jazz."

She grins, pulling me into a quick hug. "That's it. Now go home and get some rest. And maybe think about texting that current obsession of yours."

"He's not my anything," I call after her, but she's already out the door, leaving me alone with my thoughts again.

As I walk toward the bus home, the cool night air clearing my head a bit, I allow myself to really think about Odin—not just as a project partner or an inconvenience to my plans, but as a person. What must he be going through right now? His whole future, everything he's worked for, is suddenly up in the air. And yet, when I saw him, he still managed to be kind, even in the face of my spectacular social ineptitude.

He must have been on some intense pain meds, based on how his pupils looked in the hospital. Not that I was looking at his pupils at all.

I think about his family, too. The way they rally around him, their love and concern palpable even to an outsider like me. It makes me ache a little for reasons I don't want to examine too closely. Fern's always talking about that family, how tight they are, and how they support each other. It helps when you always have your basic needs met and don't have to panic about money constantly.

And I'm going to become a person who works to change that! We can become a country where everyone has that sort of chance, dang it. I just need to finish this last month of college and step into my true purpose: Thora Janssen— International Policy Researcher. Rhodes Fellow. All around policy changemaker.

And then, unbidden, my mind drifts to less...academic thoughts. Like how Odin looked unfairly attractive even in a hospital gown. Or how his hand felt when our fingers brushed as I offered him a cookie. I shake my head, trying to dislodge these unhelpful thoughts. This is ridiculous. I do not have time for a crush.

As I reach my parents' house, I make a decision. I'll find a way to make this right. To balance my coursework with human decency. To be worthy of a Rhodes Scholarship and, more importantly, deserving of Odin's forgiveness.

But as I crank up my air purifier and climb into bed, my last thoughts before sleep claims me are of piercing blue eyes and a smile that makes my heart do somersaults.

I am so, so screwed.

# CHAPTER 5
# ODIN

I SIT in the front of Mom's car after getting wheeled out to the curb, cramming cookies in my mouth and staring out the window as she drives me home. When we get to my apartment, we realize it's not an accessible building. There are stairs everywhere.

I stand outside the door, one leg resting on the knee roller, one hand on the handlebars, the other clutching that damn tin of cookies.

Mom stares at the steps into the building and the stairwell up two floors to the apartment I share with my brother and cousins. "Odin, I'm so sorry." Mom gestures at the stairs like she is the architect or something. "This isn't accessible at all, is it? Not even a ramp…"

I sniff. This building is for student-athletes, so it makes sense that there's a minimum expectation of walking ability. Mom sighs. "I'll run up and grab your brother, okay? We'll get you inside."

I have no idea what the plan is to get me upstairs. I'm not crawling up the steps. I guess I'd let Gunnar give me a piggy-back ride. Lord knows I've carried his drunk ass up to our apartment that way before.

Gun and Stellan make their way outside, along with Mom, who looks like she wants to cry. Gunny claps a hand on my shoulder. "This sucks, bro," he offers. I grunt at him.

Mom fiddles with her car keys. She's double-parked outside the building, and people are starting to stare at us as traffic backs up behind her black SUV. "I'm just going to move the car, and I'll come in with your things, okay?"

I wave a hand at her because what do I care where she parks?

Stellan walks around my knee roller, checking out the foam pad where I'm supposed to rest my cast. I can put weight on my knee, but not under any circumstances, my foot or lower leg.

Gunnar points a thick finger at me and says, "I assume you don't want me to throw you over my shoulder?"

"Fuck you." I flip my brother the bird because this is how we communicate our love when our parents aren't around.

Stellan scratches his chin, squinting at the apartment entrance. "I think we can hop this together," he says.

Gunnar nods. "Odin, you put your left hand on the banister, right arm around me, and we'll hop you up. Stelly can carry this contraption."

"Why do you get to help him hop?" Stellan is now put out over not being chosen to help his invalid cousin up the stairs. I groan and finagle my roller toward the banister, testing my weight on the creaky railing.

"I'm his brother, asshole. When your brother gets hurt, you can help him hop."

Stellan flicks Gunnar in the ear. "Don't say that about getting hurt, man. You're going to jinx us."

I kick the knee roller away with a growl. "You guys going to fight all day or help me inside?"

"Sorry, bro." Gunnar slides up against my side. "I won't even pinch you this time. Or tickle you. Maybe." He wedges his shoulder under mine and locks an arm around my waist. We're about the same height, so it works okay. After a few days lying in a hospital bed, I'm weaker than I want to admit, so I give him my weight and hop up the few stairs to the apartment door.

I use the roller to get down the hall and then rely on Gunny again to get up two flights of stairs to our apartment, which I realize I'll have to leave every morning for PT. "How is this shit going to work," I ask the room at large.

There's an uncomfortable silence as my brother and cousin shift their weight and stare at their backpacks. They need to get to class. Mom walks in the door carrying the football uniform I forgot I was wearing when they rushed me to the hospital. Someone stuffed it in a clear plastic trash bag, which is probably where it will stay. I'm not sure what happened to my pads or helmet. I guess I have to return the jersey to the athletic department. That's a problem for another day.

"What do you need to get comfortable, Odin?" Mom sets the bag on the ground and looks around the apartment. There are a lot of cardboard boxes stacked all over since Wyatt is moving out, but the place is otherwise not too messy—for once. Typically, Mom is full of jokes and comments about our filthy kitchen and toilets, but today, she wrings her hands together and stares at me, her eyes shiny, like she's trying not to cry.

You and me both, Mom.

"I'm just going to bed," I say, testing out the knee roller on the apartment carpet. I glide my ass to my room and am glad to see I fit through the door pretty easily. From there, I quickly hobble into my bed; once settled, I realize I didn't set myself up with water, snacks, or anything. "Can you bring me my cookies, Mom?"

I'm 22 years old, asking my mother to bring me a box of

cookies. But she does it, smiling. She sets the tin on my night-stand along with a glass of water and a clementine. I know we don't keep fresh fruit in the apartment, so this is clearly pity fruit. "Isn't this for your snack later?" I reach for the cookies but point at the orange.

She smiles. "Your father can bring me another one. He likes visiting my chambers."

"Gross, Mom." My parents are always making weird sex jokes about her judge's office.

She ruffles my hair and kisses the top of my head. She reaches into her pocket and sets a few pill bottles on the nightstand. "I'll call around four if I don't hear from you that you took these, okay?"

I nod and adjust the covers. I hear her talking softly to Gunnar, and then I hear the apartment door close. I'm alone. I cuddle the tin of cookies to my chest like it's a throw pillow. Did Thora really come to the hospital to give me shit about a group project? I guess she at least brought me some cookies. I stare at the phone number on the lid of the tin. Should I thank her? Or give her shit for being a jerk about schoolwork?

I decide to send her a text.

ME

Hey

THORA FROM CLASS

Sorry. Wrong number.

ME

It's Odin [deer emoji]

THORA FROM CLASS

Oh shit. Sorry! How are you? I'm so sorry I was such a jerk yesterday. There you were in the hospital after surgery, and I was bugging you about class. Don't even worry about it. I'll write the paper and put both our names on it.

I stare at her message. It's not like I ever care much about my classwork. Under ordinary circumstances, I'd happily take credit for her work and be done with it. But nothing is ordinary anymore. Before I can think too hard about it, I write back:

> No way. I can't have you putting my name on something I haven't even read. What if you do a terrible job?

THORA FROM CLASS

Okayyyy well…are you going to be able to work on it? From the hospital?

ME

> I'm home now, actually. And I no longer have football practice eating into my spare time, so…

THORA FROM CLASS

So?

ME

> So why don't you come over? We can work on it this afternoon when my pain meds wear off, and I can think clearly.

THORA FROM CLASS

Today? Are you sure? We have a few weeks.

ME

> I literally have nothing else to do.

This is partly a lie. I'm supposed to schedule meetings with my academic advisors, coach, the financial aid people, and my athletic trainers. I have a whole team of people who care about their investment in my attendance at this school as a football player. But here I am, for a change, doing something as a student.

ME

Bring more cookies.

I toss the phone on my nightstand without waiting for her reply, and I roll over and finally grab a few hours of sleep.

# CHAPTER 6
## THORA

"I'M SUPPOSED to go to his apartment." I blurt this into my phone with no preamble, but Fern is used to this style of communication from me.

"Well, it's not like he can get to you very easily," Fern replies, her voice far off like she has me on speaker while she's doing other things. Which I'm sure she is. We graduate in less than a month, and Fern leaves immediately to go to grad school in London. I will be in Pittsburgh without her for the entire summer before my fellowship starts at Oxford. Fern continues, explaining, "Wyatt told me Odin is on a ton of pain meds. Or he's supposed to be, but he's being stubborn about taking them, so he mostly lies around moaning and growling."

I immediately picture him moaning, not in pain but in pleasure. The man is smoking hot, but he knows that. He's a Division One athlete. Of course, he knows his body is a wonderland. I clear my throat and check the time. I have a few minutes before my history class. "So, do I just go over there and sit on his bed with him?"

"They have chairs," Fern says. She's basically married to

Odin's cousin Wyatt, who lived in the same apartment until he left to play professional soccer abroad. She's probably had sex on the chairs over there. I shove that thought away and croak out an affirmative sound.

————

Sitting in class, I pay half attention to my professor as I stress about going to Odin Stag's and trying to work on our class project. It was easy to picture him naked and move on when we were just regular classmates. He doesn't even sit near me. But, our professor assigns random pairings for each project and it was my turn to get paired up with the athlete in class. I really thought he'd be glad to have me do the whole thing. I know he wasn't serious when he said it might not be good. I mean, I don't want to sound cocky, but I'm a Rhodes scholar. I don't do bad work.

Odin's apartment is near the bar where I work so it's nothing for me to go over there in between class and my shift. I'll have to figure something out for dinner. These mundane thoughts distract me from all the bigger stressors weighing down on me lately. I've spent my whole damn life trying to change my circumstances, and I'm right on the cusp of succeeding. I can smell it above the exhaust fumes and alley pee in Odin's neighborhood.

I don't know how I ended up driven to excel academically in a house full of long-time service workers and people with an addiction. My dad's been on house arrest for months now, and Mom has a record, too, making it hard for her to get any sort of job that offers a decent wage.

My grad fellowship is meant to be me studying international policies around parole and incarceration. Everyone from my neighborhood seems to cycle through generational patterns of poverty, petty crime, and dispropor-tionate consequences.

But just winning this fellowship isn't enough. I know enough about the world to know the deck is stacked against me. I don't have a passport yet. I'm saving up my tips to deal with that and get myself a laptop and a new wardrobe. Oh, and a flight. I have to really save up to afford a flight overseas.

Ugh, it's all swimming to the surface again and making me twitchy, so I bite my lip and walk faster. If I can make headway on this class project with Odin, I won't feel strangled by all this other stuff.

Someone holds the door open for me at Odin's building, and I walk up and knock on their apartment door. I hear a grunting sound from inside that might be an invitation to enter. I hope it wasn't a sex noise. I tentatively open the door and see Odin sprawled on the couch, his booted foot elevated on the arm, long, hairy legs sticking out from a pair of athletic shorts that cling to all the lumps and bumps around his crotch.

Nope, not gonna stare at his crotch. I move my eyes to his face and smile. "Ready to get to work?"

He frowns at me, almost like he forgot I was coming over, but he shrugs, and I make my way over to the armchair next to his head. "We need a right-sized topic that we can write about for five pages. I was thinking we should argue for increased government funding for colleges and universities."

He shakes his head. "You're not going to just boss me around and bulldoze the whole report, Thora." I...like how my name sounds coming out of his mouth. I like it too much. "That topic sucks."

I scoff at him. "Maybe because you never had to worry about paying for school, Mr. Scholarship."

He arches a brow at me. "Pretty sure Fern told me you're on scholarship, too, Ms. Bossy."

"I'm not bossy." He stares at me. "I'm assertive. I have to be. People think they can run over me otherwise."

He snorts. "Because you're pint-sized."

"We can't all be six-foot-eighteen." I wish I had a pillow to swat him with. I actually glance around his living room, looking for one, but they're all either under his head or the heel of his boot. I take a deep breath. "This isn't productive. What topics would *you* like to pursue for our paper, Stag?"

He stares at the ceiling and laces his fingers together behind his head, which makes his t-shirt ride up and shows me a tan, smooth expanse of belly skin looking taut above the waist of his shorts. "We should still do something related to low-resource students and school funding." His sentence surprises a huff out of me and he squints. "You don't think I know a million guys on the football team who are only here because of sports? Trust me, nobody is telling these guys they're smart like you."

"I...never considered the people on athletic scholarships."

Another sniff from Odin. "You and a lot of other people. I'd love to have time to take harder classes. We spend almost 40 hours a week on football stuff and still have to take 12 credits."

The fridge hums to life in the uncomfortable silence as we both realize I've been sanctimonious. Again. "Okay, so what's the topic, then? Pathways to college for kids with low-income families..."

"Ethics of athletic scholarships."

"Ethics of tuition at all?"

"Oh!" He sits up. "My mom loves talking about how community college should be free. I guess that's different than universities?"

"I'm not really sure, but I'll write that down. Community college should be free. We can look at what other countries do and charge?"

Odin grins. "We can work with this." We each dive into internet research, making a list of sources and potential argument topics until an alarm goes off somewhere in Odin's apartment.

He sits up and claps his hands, swinging his casted foot around to rest on the coffee table. Then he winces when I guess that puts pressure on his heel. He blows out a breath and grabs a bottle of pills from the table, swallowing some with another grimace.

I chew on the end of my pen. "You all right?"

"Don't," he says, his voice sharp. He must see me flinch because he runs a hand through his hair and fiddles with one of his earrings. I never realized he had his ears pierced before this. I wonder what else I never knew about Odin Stag. "I'm pretty beat," he says. "I'll look some stuff up and text you, and we can get started with an outline." I stare at him. "What? You didn't think I knew how to outline?"

"Are you kicking me out of your house?"

He furrows his brow. "No, but I am going to go to sleep. So, unless you want to sit here alone while I'm snoring…"

I sniff and shove my notebook back in my bag. "We really can probably do most of this over email."

"Huh-uh," he barks. "I hate that shit. Back and forth, ten thousand messages when a three-minute conversation would solve it all. We should meet in person."

"How's that going to work? We both have insane schedules." From talking with Fern, I know that Odin and all the athletes are up before dawn for weight training and have team commitments until late at night.

Odin gestures at his leg. "I don't know if anyone told you, but I'm not exactly running sprints with the starters right now."

I bite my lip, and my cheeks heat. Of course, his schedule must be a little more open now. He said as much. I try to cover. "How was I supposed to know your schedule for follow-up treatment? Anyway, *my* schedule is still insane."

"You're here now," Odin declares with another shrug. "Just come back at this time on Monday."

I snort and shake my head. "That's too far out. I will *call* you tomorrow when I get a chance."

"Fine," he says, and closes.

"Fine!" I mutter as I slam the apartment door and walk away, grinning despite myself.

# CHAPTER 7
## ODIN

I HAVEN'T BEEN to class since my injury. How long has it been? A week? A year? I only left the apartment once to follow up with my surgeon, and it was such a debacle getting up and down the stairs that I haven't bothered since.

So, I don't know why I'm up and dressed and slithering down the stairs on my ass to wheel myself to this arguments class. I pretty much decided to withdraw from the semester and finish later. I have nothing else to do in the fall. Except if I withdraw now, that leaves Thora without a partner.

We've hung out together daily, working on this project when she has time between her classes and her grueling schedule at the bar. She wants to take over and do this whole project herself, on her timeline, and...I don't want to let her do that for some reason. The girl gets under my skin. So maybe I'm dragging myself up Forbes Avenue to prove something to her.

I growl in frustration when a car is parked too close to the corner, blocking the curb cut, and I can't get my knee roller up without a hassle. Some jagoff honks at me when the light turns, and I question every one of my life choices to date.

Despite all of this, I'm always on time for class and events.

People think I'm really laid back, but I guess growing up in a house with world-class athlete parents rubbed off on me. I'm disciplined about my schedule when I care, which I did until I got hurt.

I park my roller in the back corner of the class and wedge myself into the too-small desk, sprawling my cast into the aisle but unable to do anything about it. Thora walks in, and I watch her eyes widen at the sight of me. She hurries to a desk in front of me and sinks into the seat, her dark hair flouncing over her tiny shoulders. She really is a small person.

"What are you doing here?" She hiss-whispers like it's some secret or like I'm an intruder.

I shrug. "Attending class? With my project partner?"

Her eyes roll hard enough to make me dizzy. "Aren't you supposed to be in bed with your foot elevated or something?"

I waggle my eyebrows at her. "You like thinking of me in bed, Janssen?" An adorable flush blooms across her cheeks as the professor makes his way into the room and dumps his stuff on the lectern he never uses. Professor Ferda likes to sit on the edge of a table, facing us but still looming above us. Except I'm pretty much at eye level with him, sitting. Not that I've made a habit of making eye contact.

"All right, scholars," he says, clapping his hands. "We've got what? A week left together? By now, you've got all the basic concepts for forming effective arguments, persuading an audience, and utilizing a call to action, right? Right?" He waits for us all to murmur at him, and he smiles. "So, I'm going to give you all a chance to workshop your final presentations. If you're not already, please move to sit with your partner. You'll have five minutes to organize your outlines, and then I will have you swap with another group."

Professor Ferda hands out a worksheet with things we are supposed to look for in each other's outlines. I'm one thousand percent certain Thora, and I have all this shit in place already. The last draft of the outline she sent me was so detailed I spent a half hour just crossing things out and whittling it all down.

Which she points out when she flings our printed outline onto her desk and glares at me. "What's with all this? Those were good ideas."

"We would have gone over the time limit," I insist. "It's more refined this way—three main arguments. We can't get into the weeds talking about socialized healthcare and paid parental leave when we only have ten minutes. We need to stick to education."

Thora frowns. I could already tell she was one of those people who spews out the entire context of every possible angle before she can get to the meat of an argument. Except when she's sparring with me, it seems. And I kind of like that she gives me shit on a regular basis. Who shows up in someone's hospital room to yell at them about group work? This girl.

"The free healthcare is important, though. It shows the Scandinavian values."

"Are we talking about the merits of socialism, or are we talking about free college?" I raise a brow and cross my arms.

She huffs. "They're the same thing." She crosses her arms.

I'm about to tell her she's absolutely incorrect when Professor Ferda stops by my desk. "Hey, Odin." His voice is saccharine, like I'm seven and scraped my knee. "I was sorry to hear about your injury. I wasn't expecting you back in class after your advisor reached out."

I shrug. "I haven't talked to him this week. I would never leave Thora high and dry." I wink at her, and that seems to piss her off, so I file that away to do it again sometime.

Professor Ferda nods and purses his lips before saying, "Okay, great. Well, why don't you two switch papers with Jean and Malcolm?"

I let Thora scribble all over the other group's notes, watching as she mutters to herself the whole time. Class ends, and we get our paper back with only a few smiley faces in the margins. I can tell this bothers Thora, so I thank Jean and slide the paper into my sweatpants pocket. "Where to now?" I ask Thora, and she rears her head in confusion.

"Um, I work."

I frown. I hadn't considered that she had shit to do and wouldn't just come back to my place for more arguments. If I'm really honest, I want her near my bed in case I convince her to join me in it. I scratch my chin. "At the bar?" She nods. "But it's slow during the day if you want to finish our sources in between customers?"

I shrug. "I guess I'll be a barfly then. I've never been to a bar during daylight hours..."

"I can't believe this is how you're going to spend your afternoon." She tugs on her backpack straps.

I realize I haven't exactly told her that this paper is officially the only thing I have going on until I start physical therapy. I get myself situated on the knee roller.

She winces. "Are you going to sit there and bug me?"

"Ah, so I bug you? Sounds interesting." Veins start pulsing in her neck, and I laugh. "I'll sit on a bar stool, and eat some soup or something, and work on our bibliography."

Thora bites her lip, which is probably the only plump thing on her body, and I stare as she works her teeth along the rosy, sensitive skin. "I guess that's okay."

I start rolling back down Forbes, and she walks beside me. "Don't you usually work evenings?"

She sighs. "I work whenever I can get in there. You know I'm moving to the UK this fall, right?" I shake my head. She hums. "Fern and I both are. She's there long term but I'm just there for a year. And I need so much stuff I can't afford yet." She pauses while I navigate a curb cut, successfully this time.

"You probably don't care about my airfare or professional wardrobe."

"I care. I'm not an asshole."

"Oh, no, you're renowned for your benevolence." Thora laughs. "What do they say about you? That you rack people up by the horns or something?"

"Well, nobody's going to say that ever again, are they?"

Thora stares at me with her mouth hanging open. "Oh my god, Odin. I'm so sorry. I keep doing that to you. How can you stand me?"

"I'm not really sure I can," I joke. We get to the bar, and she holds the door open. I'm happy to see this place has a ramp from the curb. I guess the owners want everyone to be able to access their cheap beer and fried food. I make my way to the stool at the end of the bar, and Thora walks behind it, tossing her bag somewhere and tugging on a black apron.

"What'll it be, Stag?"

I consider this. She's right about the meds not mixing with liquor. But this place serves all kinds of fried food I'm never allowed to eat while training. And I'll never have anyone telling me what to eat again. I slap the sticky wood surface of the bar. "Bring me the app platter."

She frowns. "That's meant to serve four people."

"App. Platter." I enunciate each syllable and pop all the p's until Thora laughs and shakes her head. I watch as she types in my order and then hurries to serve some preppy kid who thinks he's cool because winks at the bartender.

She walks off to pour his beer, and I glare at him when he sets a crumpled dollar in a ring of condensation on the bar. He walks off with his beer as Thora heads to the kitchen, presumably for my food, and I reach in my wallet for a five, placing that guy's shitty tip along with my addition on a drink napkin, nice and smooth and dry.

When Thora sets the food in front of me, she sees the tip,

and a smile spreads wide across her face. She folds the bills neatly and adds them to the jar by the register.

I eat all the fried food, knowing it will make my gut churn. It takes me five minutes to type up our sources for our essay, so I take my time and watch her work. I confer with her between customers and add some stuff that we can use for our presentation to a list on my phone.

I was going to pester her into returning to my apartment after her shift, but I'm exhausted between leaving the house and eating all the heavy food. I text my cousins to come get me and leave a twenty folded neatly by my plate.

I force myself to walk away because if she sees me, she will refuse the tip, and I want her to have it.

———

When I get back to the apartment, there's an envelope sitting on my pillow. I frown at it because the edge is ripped like one of these buffoons opened my mail. I sit on the edge of my bed and chill my irritation when I see the letter is only addressed to "Mr. Stag," which could really be anyone here.

My guts churn when I see that it's a check from the college football video game that made me into a character. I knew this was coming, but it still feels like shit to see it sitting here. What the fuck am I supposed to do with this money? What kid wants me in their damn video game anymore?

I consider ripping up the damn thing, but that feels disrespectful to Thora, who is still working behind the bar and will be for hours. I shove the check and the envelope in my desk drawer and pop a pain pill, hoping for sleep.

# CHAPTER 8
## THORA

"THORA! GET THE DOOR!" My dad bellows from the living room, where I'm sure he's sprawled on the couch from the night before. Chances are pretty high that he was drinking, but chances are also pretty high that his probation officer won't stop by today to check.

I brace myself to dash through the cloud of cigarette smoke before it occurs to me that people don't usually knock on the door at eight in the morning. I poke my head out of my bedroom. "Are you sure it's not the P.O.?"

Dad snarls, and I sigh, grabbing my backpack. I try to spend as little time as possible at my parents' house and even less time away from the air purifier and dryer sheet haven I rigged up in my bedroom. I know I can't do anything about having grown up poor, but I sure can try to keep the cigarette smoke smell away from my clothes, hair, and school supplies.

I shoulder the heavy bag and peek through the smeared glass pane on the door, shocked to see Odin Stag waving up at me from the sidewalk. Yanking open the door and stepping outside, I hiss, "What are you doing here? How did you know where I live?"

Odin waves at a black vehicle idling in the street, and the

driver peels off with a deliberate screech of the tires. Odin shakes his head. "A, I got a ride from my brother so I could go over our bibliography before it's due today, and B, you shared your dot with me the other day."

I furrow my brow. "I shared my dot?"

He shrugs, adjusting his giant frame on his knee roller device. "On your phone. The tracking thing."

I lean against the stoop, still wondering how he managed to knock on the door without climbing the four concrete steps. Maybe his brother knocked for him? "I never shared my location with you."

Odin grins, one of his earrings twinkling in the morning sun. "It's possible. I asked Fern where you live."

"Why would you do that? She would have told me." I didn't realize Fern chats with the Stag family, especially since Wyatt moved out of the country.

Odin rolls closer to me. "Like I said, I wanted to talk about the project before class, but you weren't answering your phone."

I slide the device in question from my coat pocket, and sure enough, I missed a zillion texts from Odin and Fern, as well as a few calls. "Oh, sorry. I set it to do not disturb when I was at the bar, and I guess I forgot to turn it back on."

"Seems unlike you, Janssen." He winces, and I realize he must be uncomfortable. I bite my lip. "I, um, can't really invite you up." I gesture vaguely at my parents' row home. "But we're just a few blocks from Constellation Coffee if you want to go sit and talk?"

He checks a very fancy watch and shakes his head. "Nah, we better start moving to campus. Don't tell me you walk the whole way from here?"

I scoff at him. "I take the bus. Do you not know about the bus?"

He shrugs. "Never had to worry about it before this." He waves a hand at his foot. I think about how close his apartment is to campus and remember again that I've had an unconventional education. That's why I usually only hang out with Fern. She gets it. She lived at home all four years, too, and we were queens of finding library space to camp out on long stretches between classes. We know where all the free food is around campus and the best places to nap without worrying that anyone will snatch our bags.

"Come on, big guy." I start walking up the hill toward Penn Ave. "I'll show you the splendors of the 93 bus." He rolls alongside me quietly, grunting a bit at the rough spots in the sidewalk. I slow my stride and absolutely do not stare at his ass in his gray sweatpants. I also don't admire his shoulder muscles, obvious and visible even in his hoodie. "You've got to be six feet tall," I mutter, and he laughs.

"That's what you're thinking about right now?" Odin growls as his roller catches on a tree root. He hoists the device up and over the uneven surface and says, "I'm six-four. And before you ask, so is my dad, and all my brothers are right around that range. We grow 'em big in the Stag family." I'm treated to a wink that sets my pants on fire, and I know this guy knows exactly how good he looks, but I am swooning like a jersey-chasing fan regardless. If I were the sort of person who went to sporting events, I'd be screaming over the railing right now at half-time, begging Odin to fire a t-shirt cannon my way.

I try to cover my ogling by explaining, "I was just thinking about how we will get you inside the bus. Some of them have a ramp that flips out, but some just…" I try to demonstrate how the buses sort of squat to let old ladies step aboard.

"Don't worry about me," he says. I nod and point at the bench inside the bus shelter. He shakes his head. "We can stand. I'm serious. I have enough people worrying about me and treating me like an invalid. Talk to me about our sources for class."

I'm about to tell him about conference proceedings I

downloaded from some university in Portugal when I spot a bright red bus chugging up Penn Ave from the Strip District. I wave at the driver, who stops and stares at Odin. Does the driver recognize him? I guess so in this sports-obsessed town. The bus beeps and squats down, and I don't know if I should get in first and help him or...actually, I have no idea what to do because there's no way I could lift him or anything. He gestures for me to get on, and I do.

He heaves his knee roller in the door, and I grab it with one hand as he muscles the rest of himself into the bus. He's not even breathing heavily. The driver and I both look at him, impressed. I shake myself out of my stupor and tap my student ID on the fare box. Odin arches a brow and fishes in his pocket for his wallet, clearly unused to having his ID at the ready to gain access to buses and, probably, dining halls.

Everyone on board watches as he rolls down the aisle to the accessible seating. I stand in front of him, and he scowls, clearly grappling with some sense of chivalry and the dueling reality of his temporary impairment. I cross my arms over my chest and frown at him until he sinks into the seat, tucking the roller in between his enormously long legs. I consider sitting on his lap, on his good leg, obviously. Would he even notice my weight? I shake my head as the bus chugs forward. I steady myself on the pole by Odin's head, and he glances up at the strap hanging from the bar far above my reach. "Neither of us is well-suited for this," he says with a shake of his head.

I shrug. "Beats walking, I guess."

————

Once on campus, the sidewalks are better maintained, and the buildings have ramps and elevators. We get to class a little bit early and settle into seats in the back of the room. I pull out my ancient laptop and open my mouth to tell Odin about the new source.

"What the hell is that thing?" Odin points at my laptop, which whirs noisily. I glare at him. "Is that a telegraph machine? Why is it so big?"

I punch him in the arm, which stings because his body is pure muscle. He shakes his head and removes a shiny, light-weight laptop from his bag. "You said something about Portugal?"

I can smell him seated this close together. His laundry detergent smells expensive, and there's a whiff of either hair gel or deodorant or maybe cologne with an alpine scent. I like it…too much. I guess it's fine that I'm attracted to him. What straight girl in Pittsburgh wouldn't be? I can give him a huff and work on this project and still achieve what I need to get out of here in a few months.

"Did you just sniff me?" He leans close to my ear to ask this, and his breath melts over my cheek and neck like honey. Shit, this is bad.

"Yes." I turn to face him, meeting his blue eyes with my dark gaze. "You stink."

A laugh rumbles out of him as the professor walks into the room. "You lie, Thora."

# CHAPTER 9
# ODIN

MY TINY LITTLE research partner is into me, which is great because she's hot. I don't see an issue, apart from the fact that my life is ruined and my foot is in a giant cast. And, also, I can't move very well. I pay minimal attention to the teacher through the rest of class, demand that Thora come to my house whenever she's done with her shit today, and I wheel myself toward home.

Only I don't get very far because my athletic advisor appears out of nowhere, jogging toward me on Forbes Avenue. "Odin! Hold up, please."

I squint at him, backlit by the sun. Behind him, construction cranes work on new classroom buildings, likely partly funded by revenue from television contracts for my football team. Meech looks pissed, which is fair. I've been blowing him off for a few weeks. "Hey, Meech."

Demetrius Thomas is in charge of keeping the entire football team in line—academically, behaviorally, you name it. Most of the time, he's worried about our academic eligibility to play ball, but I suspect his vigorous chase down the city streets today is more related to scholarship shit. He wheezes a bit, holding his hand on his chest as he catches his breath.

"Been trailing you since the Cathedral of Learning, kid. Your brother tell you I came by your house?"

"He might have said that. A lot of people have been stopping by." This is always true—girls with flowers. Football fans wanting to know what my injury means for their fantasy draft. My coaches.

Meech leans against the window of the Seven-11. "You're supposed to be withdrawn from school, Stag. Medical withdrawal. What are you doing going to class?"

I sniff. This guy is still acting like I will play football in the fall for my final year of eligibility. Meanwhile, I'm months away from even walking again. Exactly one running back has ever come back from a ruptured Achilles tendon, and he was already on a pro team when he got injured. I stare at Meech and lean on my knee roller. "I have something I need to do next week, then I'll sign the forms."

Meech arches a dark brow above an angry set of eyes. "You need to address this before finals. You haven't been going to class, Odin. Failing out is different from a legitimate withdrawal for an injury."

There's no way I'm pulling from this final presentation now. Thora would be smug about doing it all herself, and she'd fuck it all up, trying to argue the entire internet. I'm not sure why I care so much about this stupid assignment, but I also know she's got a lot riding on her perfect grade point average. "I don't know what to tell you, man. I have a presentation I have to do next week. I will roll directly from there to the registrar's office. Or yours, if you can handle that stuff."

"What day next week?" He crosses his arms over his chest, standing over me. Meech played ball back in college, too. Didn't go pro. Now spends his days wrangling assholes like me. I'm actually pretty good. I don't get my girlfriends pregnant. I don't blow my rent money on tattoos. My big annoying flaw is staying enrolled in school when I ought to bow out.

"Tuesday," I tell him. "I'll be done by ten." I turn around and roll toward my house before he can shout after me. I don't think he follows me, but I don't check.

———

It's obvious my parents were at the apartment. By the time I get myself back up the stairs, the fridge has been stocked with soup and grilled chicken. There's a bowl on the coffee table full of little baggies of roasted almonds, and approximately 700 bananas teeter on a rack on the counter. I cram almonds into my mouth and play video games until a tap on the door announces the arrival of Thora Janssen. I look at my watch. I've been ignoring the world for hours. I guess my brothers and my cousin Stellan all went straight from class to workouts.

"Come in," I shout, hoping I left the door unlocked.

She slips in and sinks onto the couch beside me. "God, what a day. I was at the law clinic this afternoon. You wouldn't believe the things human beings do to one another, Odin. It's horrifying."

"I forgot you work at the law clinic." I adjust my posture so I'm facing her as best I can.

Thora nods. "I mean, it's volunteering. But yes."

I nod, too. "Yeah. You helped Wyatt get his shit together. Turned his whole life around."

Thora purses her lips. "Honestly, I just check people in for the most part. It's people like your mom who are actually doing the work. They're the ones who change lives."

"Okay, but you're there helping. Someone has to check people in. Right?"

She makes a face at me, like she wants to stick out her tongue or leave rather than accept appreciation. I grunt. She must think I'm a gorilla. Maybe I'm just hungry. I hear a sound and stare at her. "Was that your stomach?"

Thora looks sheepish. "Yeah. I'm going to grab dinner after we finish our draft."

I frown and shake my head. "We should eat. My parents brought soup."

"Soup?" She looks like she never heard of it before. Or maybe she's not used to parents who make food. Her family sounded bitchy when I knocked on her door this morning.

"Yeah. I'll share if you heat it up for us."

Her face lights up. "Deal. You've got clean bowls and stuff, right?"

I flip her the bird, and she cackles, yammering at me about mean landlords and terrible employers while she heats soup on the stove.

She carries two steaming bowls to the couch, a pair of spoons tucked into her back jeans pocket. I stare at them. Am I supposed to reach in and pluck them out, thus touching her ass? Does she want me to touch her ass? She was ogling mine earlier…

"Hello? McFly?" Thora waves a hand in my face. She sets the bowls on the coffee table beside my boot cast and must have been asking me something.

"Say again? Sorry."

"I was asking where you keep the napkins." She glances around and, spotting a roll of paper towels, strides toward them to rip off a few. The question about the spoons is answered when she pulls them out with one hand, tucks a paper towel into my hoodie pocket, and hands me a bowl of soup, all in one smooth motion. Seeing my impressed face, Thora smiles. "Bartender skills." She grabs her soup and sits beside me, close enough that I can smell floral perfume above the garlicky aroma of my dad's minestrone. "Oh shit, this is good. Your parents made this?"

I nod, slurping some of the broth. A surge of emotion hits me along with the flavors on my tongue. Dad started cooking when he retired from pro hockey to raise me and my brothers.

Not sure why I feel like sharing, but I blurt, "My dad stayed home to support my mom's judicial career." Thora's eyes go wide. I take another bite of soup, and she matches my movements, silently waiting for me to tell her more. "Mom's on the Commonwealth Court now, but she did family court for a long time. She's Juniper—"

Thora gasps, cutting me off. "Juniper Jones, is your *mom?* Holy shit. She's a hero. I met her at the student law clinic a bunch of times. She's *amazing.* She remembered that I was going for the Rhodes scholarship. She's your mom? Of course, she is…"

I eat more soup, but I'm not sure how to respond to all of that. I'm more used to people freaking out about my dad. I guess there are more sports fans in my social circle than…are court fans even a thing? Law fans? "You want to be a lawyer?"

Thora nods and sets her empty soup bowl on the coffee table with a clang. "I'm definitely going to be a lawyer. I told you why I'm going to England, right? To study international approaches to child welfare and recidivism for nonviolent crimes? Your mom is the star of a bunch of case studies I've read for class. Didn't she start in sports law? That always seemed out of character to me…"

I finish my soup and stretch forward, batting Thora's hand away when she tries to help me reach the coffee table. I might not be able to do much, but I can set my own fucking bowl down when I'm done eating. I pop my evening pain meds into my mouth, swallow, and explain, "Mom had to switch jobs sort of abruptly, and my Uncle Tim had an opening." I turn to face Thora, adjusting my cast to sit sideways on the couch. "Can we be done talking about my family now?"

"Hm. Sure." Thora reaches for her backpack and pulls out the laptop, which is really more of a barely portable desktop machine on its last legs. "Let's crank out a draft."

———

She has, of course, written most of it already and included way too many footnotes and parenthetical asides, which I delete until she acknowledges that my version is much more streamlined and effective. We get most of a draft down while she gets us more soup. By the time she leans back with her hand on her belly, I'm exhausted but still hungry. This would be the perfect time for me to make a joke about eating my next course…between her legs. But it wouldn't be a joke. Not for me, anyway. I scratch my neck. "I have to do something else. My head is spinning." I make my way to my feet, and Thora looks concerned. When I frown at her, she schools her features. "I'm not fragile, you know."

"Ha! I can see that. I just…want to be helpful. That's all."

I rest my knee on the couch, so I'm not putting weight on my bad foot; like a good patient, I scratch my neck. I haven't shaved in a while. Maybe I'll grow a beard now that I don't have to wear a helmet over it. She continues to stare at me like I'm fragile until I stretch and sit back down on the couch. "All right," she says, looking at her phone. "Let's map out a plan to finalize this and practice our oral presentation." She clacks away, sending notifications to me, which I ignore as the meds kick in and begin to dull the throbbing in my lower leg.

I must be dozing off because Thora startles me by resting a hand on my shoulder. "Hey," she says, and I don't like the soothing tone in her voice. I like it better when she's mean to me. "I'm going to head out."

I try to respond, but all that comes out is a grunt. She stands up and then bends to grab her backpack, and my lizard brain overtakes my rational mind, and I rest my palm on her backside. I don't squeeze or rub. I…hold it like a firm little watermelon, all for me

Thora glances back over her shoulder, a laugh in her eyes. "Can I help you?"

"I don't know, can you?"

She chuckles and lifts my hand from her ass, placing it on my chest and patting it in place. "Some other time, Stag, when you're less stoned."

"I'm going to hold you to that," I yell after her when she closes the apartment door. At least, I think that's what I say. I fall asleep before I can check.

# CHAPTER 10
# ODIN

BY FRIDAY, I'm barely taking any more of the pain meds, and Thora and I have hit a groove. I leave the apartment only to go to the arguments class, and she comes over between class and work. She doesn't bring up the ass incident, but she also looks away less often when I catch her staring at my junk. I'd say we're about even.

At one point, she throws her pencil across the room with a roar, and I stare at her, not used to seeing her react that strongly. "Was it something I said?"

She shakes her head. "No. I'm just being a brat. Sorry. I really wanted to work tonight, but my manager shifted me to Sunday."

I scratch my stomach, and maybe I let my shirt ride up without fixing it. "Won't you get a lot of tips during the football game on Sunday? That's a good thing, right?"

She sighs. "You're probably right. I hate being so close to finishing all this, like I can taste it, but I'm still so far off." She stares at my stomach, giving herself a long look. "You don't want to hear about this stuff."

"I don't mind. You might have noticed I don't have much going on right now."

"That's not the same as listening to your unfortunate classmate whine about growing up poor and getting shafted at work."

I grin and gesture at my crotch. "You want to talk about getting shafted, Thora? I'm very open to that." She throws a pillow at me, but I deflect and grab the one behind my head, throwing it back. She giggles. "Seriously, though. I'm very interested in that discussion if you are."

Her cheeks flush, and it's really satisfying to achieve that. She bites her lip and says, "It's not a good idea, Odin. I'm counting on this grade."

"You think I'm going to piss you off before we present next week?"

She humphs. "You already piss me off."

"Well then, what's stopping us, gorgeous?"

Thora rolls her eyes, grabs another pencil from her bag, and returns to scratching away in her notebook. I prop my laptop on a couch cushion and scroll through articles about public universities in Germany until she throws another pencil. I eye her cautiously like she's a bomb about to explode. "What now?"

"I can't concentrate."

I rub a hand across my chest, teasing, and say, "Because of my rugged good looks? It's the cast, isn't it?"

"I just really need to be done working today." Okay, so she's not in the mood to joke around. Noted.

I close the laptop, figuring I've learned all there is to know about tuition-free higher ed in Europe. Thora starts gathering her things like she's going to leave me here alone on a Friday night, and I sort of panic. "Want to play a game or something?" The question comes from nowhere, but as soon as I ask it, I realize I'm desperate for her to say yes. I can't be alone in this apartment; it's too hard to leave, and we have a really fun game shelf thanks to decades of Stag family competitiveness.

She picks up both the pencils she threw and taps one against her cheek, considering. Finally, she shrugs, and I exhale. "Sure. Like checkers or something?"

"Checkers? Are you ninety years old?" I grab my knee roller and scoot over to the shelf by the never-used dining room table. I peruse the options and grab a small box of cards from the top. "How about Taco, Cat, Goat, Cheese, Pizza?"

"What?" Thora laughs. "I don't think any of those words go together."

"Oh, they definitely do." I tip my chin at the table. "Get your ass over here and prepare to go down."

She humphs again and walks toward me, sliding past my scooter and into a chair. "You should know that I don't lose, Stag. And I never go down first."

I kick the knee roller aside and open the box, shuffling the cards as I stare into her eyes from across the table. "Care to make things interesting?"

She shakes her head. "You know I've got no money."

I shrug. "Bet something else then."

"No way." She leans toward me, trying to see the cards. "You'll just pick something dumb like making me write the whole paper for you."

"You wish. Tell me what you want if you win."

She taps her chin and stares at me, her dark hair coming loose from her ponytail, almost like her whole body is drawn toward my hands while I'm shuffling. "If I win, I get to borrow your car tomorrow so I can run errands."

I scoff. "I would have lent you the car regardless. But if that's what you really want." I start dealing the illustrated cards, face down.

"Well, what are you playing for?" She looks up at me, equal parts innocent and irritated, fierce and caring.

I deal us each a twelfth card, pressing my index finger into the top of the draw pile in the middle of the table. I stare at her as she bites her teeth into her plump lip, thinking about sinking my teeth into it. I think about how she's so bossy, so regimented, and streamlined and how much I'd love to see her frazzled. I want to see her fall apart, close her eyes, and moan. I really shouldn't ask for what I actually want if I win, but what the fuck do I have to lose? I lean back and cross my arms. "If I win, I get to watch you get off."

# CHAPTER 11
## THORA

I LICK my lips and stare into the beautiful, chiseled face of Odin Stag. Did he really just say he wants to watch me touch myself? I've never done that in front of anyone before. We've been joking about getting frisky, and it's pretty clear we're both into each other. I'm half tempted to counter-offer a full-on sex-fest if he wins, but his offer intrigues me.

"You want to watch me get off? That's it? How is that a treat for you?"

Odin's eyes fly wide, and his head draws back like I just told him the Earth is flat or something. "Are you serious? You don't understand what would be awesome about watching a woman give herself an O?"

I hitch up one shoulder and tap my fingers on the table. "Fine. If that's what you want. Easy. Tell me how to play since you won't win anyway."

Odin grins, one half of his broad mouth hooking up to the side as he explains that we are going to take turns reciting the phrases "taco," "cat," "goat," "cheese," and "pizza." Each of us will flip a card while we speak. If the card matches what we say out loud, the first person to slap the pile wins.

"And there are special cards," he explains, holding up one featuring an illustrated beaver.

"You're serious with this? I thought you'd have some sort of...sophisticated game. Are we really doing beaver faces?"

"Thora," he says, shaking his head. "This is clearly a groundhog." He knocks on the table, shows me a gorilla card, and pounds on his chest. "I don't know what gave you the idea that anyone in this apartment is sophisticated."

That draws a laugh from me, and I watch as he shuffles again. We begin. We trade wins for a few hands, each of us gently slapping the table when I say pizza and flip a pizza card, and he says goat and reveals a cute little horned critter.

But then, we stop being gentle. I see his stack of cards growing taller, and I'm a little more vigorous bringing my hand down on the top of the heap. "Yes," I hiss, ignoring the feel of my nails digging into his palm. He winces and frowns, his face going serious. With a nod, he picks up the pace.

"Goat," he says, flipping up a narwhal, and I immediately clap my hands together over my head as if they were a horn. The whole thing is absolutely absurd, and I'm having more fun than I've had in months.

We're about even when the door to the apartment opens, and his roommates limp in, groaning about practice. Stellan looks over at us, and his face brightens. "Will you deal me in?"

"No," Odin and I both yell simultaneously. He quickly flips a card, saying, "cat," and I follow rapidly with an emphatic "goat."

Odin's eyes don't leave mine as he flips cards. He must be staring at the deck with his peripheral vision, a skill he thinks he has over me as an athlete. But a bartender uses every part of her eyeballs, too. I can spot a hand waving for a drink from a crowded corner and a wedge of illustrated Swiss just as easily. "Cheese!" I wail, slamming my hand down...on top of a hunk of muscle and tendons.

"Gotta be faster if you want that sweet SUV, Jansson." Odin cackles as he straightens his cards. The other Stag guys take a seat at the table, watching us as they cram tuna in their mouths straight from the can. I don't know if I've ever been that hungry in my whole life, but I have never played Division One sports.

Odin's brother Gunnar peeks at Odin's card stack and whistles through his teeth. "Getting close to a W, bro." Gunnar looks at me. "Think you can beat him if you draw a gorilla?"

Odin and I ignore the banter and the stench of tuna, flipping cards and slapping at a pace that has my heart racing. Soon, the pile in the center of the table has at least 20 cards on it, and tension thrums thick in the air of the apartment.

Gunnar and Stellan lean forward, fascinated, but I will myself into the zone. I don't even really care about borrowing Odin's car, and I'd probably get myself off in front of him for free, if I'm honest. It's been too long since I used my pocket rocket, and I really should take care of that tonight, now that I'm all keyed up from this stupid card game.

But I want to beat him. I want to watch Odin's eyes flash in frustration when I win, and I want to see how he responds and hear what he'll say when I rub his defeat in his smug, sexy face. Is this why people play sports? God, this is invigorating. "PIZZA," I bellow, turning up a card that features a grinning kitty.

Odin purrs, although I don't think it's on purpose. His brothers elbow each other in anticipation. Whoever wins this hand will undoubtedly win the deck. I only have one card left. Odin tosses out a grinning slice of pepperoni as his deep voice shouts, "TACO," and time stops before I flip my final card.

I say the word cat but don't glance down soon enough. Odin notices the gorilla and leaps to his foot, pounding his chest before bringing his giant palm down onto the heap of cards. It's over. He's won. And he's not being coy about it. "Yessss," he roars, pumping his fists in the air.

And then, before I can register what's happening, he grabs his knee roller with one hand and hauls me over his shoulder with the other. We're gliding toward his bedroom like luggage on a baggage belt, and he dumps me onto his bed with a bounce, standing over me, chest heaving, looking sexy as fuck in the glow of his desk lamp.

I tuck my hair behind my ears and try to catch my breath as he stares at me. Odin drags a palm down his chin, chest rising and falling dramatically. "Fuck, Thora, I'm sorry. You okay?"

I laugh. "Yeah, I'm great. That was...something." Odin sits in his desk chair and kicks his knee roller away, propping his booted foot on the end of his mattress. His room is one long tube with a giant bed at the far wall and a dresser opposite the desk. There's a second door I assumed was a closet, but Odin hooks a thumb toward it and explains, "There's a bathroom if you need to get yourself ready."

"Get myself ready?" I arch a brow and lean back against his headboard. He has an actual headboard! I have a shitty twin mattress on a futon frame. I'm sure my parents dumpster dove for it when I was in elementary school.

A slow smile spreads across Odin's entire face, like a cat about to go after the leftovers from Gunnar's tuna feast. "I'm claiming my prize, Thora. So, let's see it."

I look around the room and bite my lip. "Oh. Okay, so here's the thing..."

# CHAPTER 12
## ODIN

I HAVEN'T BEEN hard since my surgery. I realize this with stunning clarity as my dick swells to life at the thought of Thora touching herself in my bed. I don't know if it's the pain meds or the brain fog, or the crushing reality of my future being destroyed, but my cock has been as limp as my prospects since my tendon exploded.

"So, here's the thing," she starts, but she doesn't look like she wants to call things off.

"Tell me, beautiful." I lean forward, hands on the arms of my desk chair, ready to jump into action.

Thora squishes her face, wrinkling her adorable nose and pursing her plump lips. "I need battery backup if this is going to work, and I didn't exactly pack for a sex party when I left for class this morning."

I nod. "Okay. Anything else?"

She looks surprised by my calm, and her eyes dart around my room like she's looking for a vibrating dildo. "Well, I usually use a book. And…"

"And?" I bring my good foot to the floor and lean forward, hands on my thighs.

She waves a hand at my bedroom door. "I actually have

the book...in my bag. I was going to read it on the bus home later."

I puff out a laugh. "You read your sex book on the bus?"

She frowns. "It has a good story, too. It just...also has good sex in it..."

"Right," I grunt and hop up to my feet, lunging for the knee roller.

"Wait. Where are you going?" Thora jumps off the bed and follows me as I make my way to the kitchen. I stretch my arm up on top of the fridge and grab the basket we keep up there as Thora scurries over to her backpack and picks it up.

Stellan, Gunnar, and my twin brothers stare at us as I wink at them and roll back to the bedroom with Thora hot on my wheels. Thankfully, they don't say anything rude that might spook her. I need this, damn it.

Thora closes the door behind her and perches on the edge of my bed, pulling a tattered paperback from her bag and dropping the bag to the floor. "Why do you have an Easter basket?" She tilts her head at the bundle on my lap, and I grin.

I crack my knuckles and explain, "My mom and aunts stock a 'safe and satisfied' kit for the apartment." I pull a strip of condoms from the top of the basket, followed by a carton of Plan B. Thora crawls up on her hands and knees to get a better look, and I let myself imagine her doing that naked. I bet I can fit her entire boob in my mouth—like a tiny apple. I decide I'll ask her to touch her nipples while she's giving me my prize in a few minutes.

I keep digging in the basket, searching for what she needs. She squints. "Is that a pamphlet for PreP?"

"Yeah." I shrug. "Why?"

She shakes her head. "Why would you guys need that? Unless..."

I clear my throat. "My brother is bi, actually, but the basket isn't just for us." I chuckle. "We're supposed to share with all our friends. Aha!" I find what I've been looking for and hold up the box.

Thora's eyes fly wide as saucers. "A cock ring?"

I nod. "A vibrating cock ring." I toss her the box. "And now it's yours, even though you don't have a cock for it."

She stares at the picture of the blue silicone ring with a vibrating nub meant for his pleasure *and* his partner's. Thora's eyes go from mine to the box and back before a crazed laugh escapes her throat. "Wow. This is unexpected, Odin."

I prop my boot back on the bed and cross my good leg over it. I lace my fingers together behind my head and lean back in my chair. "We good? 'Cause I'm ready when you are."

Thora's whole demeanor shifts. Her eyes drop to my crotch, and I let her look at the growing bulge I've got stretching out my shorts. Eventually, I'll drop a hand down there and give it a squeeze, but for now, I'm just looking forward to the show. What will it even look like when this feisty woman goes after her clit with the toy?

Thora licks her lips again and reaches for her book. It falls open to a page she appreciates, and I nod, encouraging her. "Read out loud," I demand, and she actually blushes. Again. "Oh, honey. Is that too much for you?"

Thora gives me a look and tugs down the zipper on her jeans. I grab my phone and put on a playlist at max volume. Even still, I hear the hum as she activates the toy, which thankfully came charged in the box because I was probably going to cry if we had to wait an hour for it to juice up. She adjusts her posture and leans back against the headboard, which lifts her tits a little more and gives me a nicer view of her hand moving up and down slowly inside her pants. I see that she's inside her underwear with the toy and I wonder if she's shaved bare or if she has dark pubic hair. I think about asking her, but she starts to read from the book.

*"Linus knew he shouldn't be looking through the ferns by the*

*creek, but he couldn't help himself as Sally hiked up her skirts, revealing creamy white ankles and trim calves that seemed sculpted from marble."*

"That's what turns you on?" I lean forward, adjusting my legs so I can sit up.

Thora glares. "It gets hotter. It's kind of what we're doing, actually."

"Yeah? Sally's gonna get herself off in the creek?"

Thora blushes some more and then lets out a little gasp because she's still got the toy on her clit. The book falls out of her hand, and I stretch until I can just reach it. "Let me see." I take the book and watch as Thora settles herself back on the bed. As if she can read into my fantasies, she drops one hand to her nipple, which I can see pebbled beneath her t-shirt. "Fuck," I whisper, thumbing to the dog-eared page.

"*As Linus crouched, he nearly gasped aloud when Sally's hand continued reaching higher and higher beneath her shift until she surely reached her quim. He steeled himself so he didn't fall into the water as he continued to watch the woman he had no business wanting as she touched herself in broad daylight in the creek beside her traitorous father's cabin.* Shit, Thora. What is this?" I look over the book and see her mouth half open, eyes hooded. Fuck me, I can smell her arousal, rich and spicy, behind the sweet smell of her detergent and whatever perfume she wears. "You really do get off on this, don't you, gorgeous?"

"Keep reading," she moans, the hand down her pants moving more intentionally as her nipple hand rubs faster.

"There is no fucking way I can concentrate on this book while you're making those sounds, Thora."

She opens her eyes, seemingly surprised that she has, in fact, been making noises. But oh, has she. Tiny inhalations, shuddering gasps. I memorize every single one, planning to use them all later as I brutalize my cock in the shower. "Look at you," I whisper. "You're fucking close, aren't you?"

She nods her head, and I hear a zing as she must crank up

the speed on the cock ring. I long to jump onto the bed beside her, to watch or even join in, but our bet was that she would get herself off, and the prize is so much sweeter than I ever expected. Thora Janssen has lost all her composure, all semblance of haughtiness. I might as well not even be here as she tweaks her nipple and rolls her hips, and presses that toy into her clit.

"Your pussy needs to come, doesn't she," I say, eyes fixed on the body part in question.

"Oh, god," she whines, and her hips fly up off the bed.

"Yeah, Thora, work that clit with my cock ring. Let me see, gorgeous. Fuck, that's perfect." I drop the book and press a hand to my dick as Thora comes, thrashing around on my bed with her eyes closed and her lips pressed tightly together.

I'm overcome with the need to do this again, to see if I can get her to scream. To insist that she yell my name before I let her come. I'm desperate, I realize, to touch her.

"Can I kiss you?" I'm out of the chair and perched next to her on the mattress before she can respond, needing to be closer to her body after...all of that.

Her mouth drops open, and then she presses her lips together. "I don't know, Odin..."

"Right. Right." I sit on the mattress but let my hand fall to her leg, and she seems to like that, so I rub some small circles on her jeans. Her breathing slows to regular as we sit and stare at each other.

Her hand drops to her side as she tries to calm down. I watch her chest rise and fall, slower and slower, until her breathing appears normal, and she zips up her pants. She must have clicked off the cock ring because she stares at it, silent and still and bright blue in her palm. "Where, um, should I put this?"

I close her fingers around the toy and squeeze her hand, relishing that contact with her. Shit, I'm wild for her. "It's yours, Thora. Nobody else is gonna use it."

"Not even you?" She gives me a look that makes me wish I had two good legs so I could slam her up against the door and fuck her senseless.

Eventually, she sets the toy on my pillow before gathering her hair and attempting to put it in a ponytail. "So, I need to get home."

I shake my head. "No way. It's late. I'm not letting you go out there alone, and I can't handle the stairs right now."

"Well, Mr. Bossy, I still have to run those errands tomorrow, and I want to get an early start since the buses run less often on Saturday."

I dig around in the dish on my desk until I find my keys, and I toss them to her. I'm happy to see her catch them with one hand. She's competent at this shit, and it's fucking hot. "Take the car. I can't drive it anyway."

She shakes her head. "That wasn't part of the deal. I lost the game."

I scratch my chin and stare at her, thinking. I sigh. "Okay, what if you drive me to PT, and then it's a favor for me, and you can use the car to get Sally a new shift or whatever the hell you have to do." I point to the book on my desk.

Thora's cheeks turn pink again. "Sally's shift is just fine." She stares at the wall, seeming to consider her options, and she shakes the keys in her hand. "What time do you need to be picked up? I guess I could take you. You're sure I can use the car?"

"Thora. Do I look like the kind of person who says shit I don't mean?" I cross my arms over my chest as she laughs and nods, reaching for her bag.

"Okay, okay. What time?"

I tell her to grab me at nine, and then she's gone, shoving my keys in her pocket like they belong there. I realize too late that she's forgotten the book, so I pick up where I left off, glancing through the chapter to read about Linus watching Sally whack off in the ferns. And then he can't help himself and has to touch his own turgid member, which reminds me again of the first boner I've sprung in two weeks.

I look at my bed, where the blue cock ring sits on my pillow like a kinky hotel treat. I adjust my body to my usual side of the bed, which now smells like Thora, and move the ring to my nightstand. I finish reading the chapter growing harder than before.

I slide my hand down my shorts and give my cock a squeeze, remembering how Thora looked in my bed, touching herself, pinching that tiny nipple. Fuck, she just let herself go all the way to oh-town while I watched. I give myself one more hard tug, remembering the shape of her mouth as she came, and I'm erupting all over my shirt.

I shiver with the force of my release, warm cum spurting everywhere like it's been pressurized for a month, and someone opened the faucet. That would be Thora, I guess. I yank off my shirt and use it to half-assedly clean myself up, dabbing at the white gunk on my stomach, and I realize I got jizz all over Thora's book. "Shit," I mutter, trying to mop it up with the shirt, but the ink smears, and the pages are already starting to wrinkle. "Fuck it," I mutter, reaching to turn off my light. Before I fall asleep, I vow to grab her a new copy of the book while she's out running errands in the morning.

# CHAPTER 13
## THORA

DAD GRUNTS at me from the couch as I walk in the front door on shaky legs. I'm a tiny bit nervous Odin's car will get sideswiped while parked on my street overnight, but he parks it on the street at his place, so he's probably got fancy collision insurance.

I was *not* expecting tonight to happen. I had the most intense orgasm I've ever had with another person…by myself. I'm not exactly sure what happened, to be honest. But it was hot as fuck. I give my father a tip of my chin on my way through the living room. I need to get into my room where I can breathe and call Fern.

But Dad grabs my arm on the way past. "Grab your old man a cold one while you're up?"

I press my lips together. I hate enabling him. His ankle monitor certainly doesn't impede him from walking to the kitchen, and I seriously doubt he left the couch today to move his body, look for work, or do anything at all helpful to our family. Mom has been working doubles at Ritter's since Dad got arrested, plus picking up serving shifts with Fern and me at the sports stadiums on weekends.

I sigh. I'll be out of here soon, and once I finish my fellowship, I'm not moving back into this house, no matter what. I'll have better financial prospects by then. "Sure, Dad," I mutter, hurrying to the fridge and grabbing a can of Milwaukee's Best Lite from the door, where it's crammed in among the expired mayonnaise and barbecue sauce.

I toss it to my father as I walk to the stairs, and he hollers. "You're gonna shake it up, Thora. What the hell are you doing that for?" I shake my head and hear the fizz as he opens the can regardless. I don't look back as he slurps at the foaming beer. I'm already dialing my best friend's number as I dart into my room, where I immediately spray myself with air freshener. I spend way too much on this stuff, but it's worth it to me not to have to walk around campus smelling like an ashtray. At least, I hope I can mask the stench.

Fern picks up, voice groggy. "'Lo? Thora?"

"Oh my god, you won't believe what happened," I blurt, recapping my evening with Odin.

"Wait," she interrupts. "I thought you were just going over there to work on your project?"

"Oh, we worked on it." I sink onto my bed and kick off my shoes. "And then…we did the other thing."

I hear her suck in a slow breath and whistle. "So, he didn't join in? He just watched?"

"He fucking told me what to do and sat there watching. Then I left, and I'll pick him up for PT in the morning. I have his car."

"Huh." Fern yawns, then says, "I had no idea Odin had all that in him. He usually just jokes around and plays video games when I'm over at Wyatt's."

I unhook my bra and get ready for bed. "I think maybe his injury has fucked with his head. He's different in class, too. I don't know how to explain it."

Fern tells me the whole Stag family has been worried about Odin, how he is ignoring calls from the university, and his father is worried about his mental health. It feels like a violation to hear this third hand from Odin's cousin's girlfriend. "I guess it's none of my business."

"Sorry. So, it was good? You don't usually...finish with guys."

I smile. She's right. I enjoy sex. I have a lot of it when I want to. Sometimes, I can boss a guy around and convince him to work my vibrator into the action, but more often, they get all huffy about the suggestion and leave me on the precipice to finish up later, on my own. "He seemed really into it. But what does it mean?"

"Does it have to mean anything?" Fern asks this as if she's some sort of expert rather than an intellectual currently enjoying her first-ever relationship.

"I have no actual idea," I tell her. While I'm not really one for repeats with guys, I also don't sleep with dudes I'm going to see again unless they happen to stroll back into the bar, in which case I just sort of ignore them until they go away. I sigh. "I need to try to sleep before I spend the day tomorrow with the guy."

Fern giggles. "Update me when you're back. Oh, are you getting your visa and stuff tomorrow?"

I shake my head, even though she can't see that. "Tomorrow is professional attire at the thrift shop. Maybe multiple shops since I have free transportation." We hang up the phone with me promising to share outfit photos and her promising to come with me to the post office to get my passport as soon as I have the money.

———

In the morning, I drive Odin's beast of a car back to retrieve him, enjoying the heated seats even if the SUV is too big to comfortably make tight turns in Pittsburgh's narrow streets. I shouldn't have tried to wend my way through Bloomfield back to his place, but it's too late now as I sing along to the radio while gingerly navigating the Belgian Block side roads.

Even with the fancy shocks in Odin's bougie car, I feel the rumble of the tires along the uneven granite bricks until my bones rattle. If I drove any faster, I might not need to use a vibe to get myself off. But I'm not going to think about sex in Odin's car. I'm taking him to a medical appointment.

I'm surprised to see him waiting outside when I arrive. I suspect he got his roommates to help him down all the stairs before they left for practice or whatever because Odin looks like he's been leaning on the signpost for a long time. "You're late," he says by way of greeting.

I look at the clock on his dash and furrow my brow at him. "How do you figure?"

He tosses his knee roller in the back door and hops on one foot into the passenger seat. "Because I was waiting for you." And then he flashes me a grin, so I know he's just giving me shit, but also still thinking about last night. I can just tell.

I swallow and fiddle with the rearview mirror. "Where am I taking you?"

Odin directs me south of the city to the facility where the professional football team practices. "You get to go here, too?"

He laughs. "We share field space with those guys. And medical staff, too. You can park in the close spots." Odin pulls an accessible parking tag from his hoodie pocket and clips it on the rearview mirror.

"Am I...supposed to wait for you? I don't know how long these things take."

He shrugs and fumbles as he tries to hop around and open the door to get his roller. I unbuckle and race around the car to help him, which seems to frustrate him. "I got it," he snaps. And then his face sags. "Sorry. This is my first appointment. It'll be like two hours. You don't have to wait, but it would be great if you could be back around eleven."

I shrug and hold the scooter in place while Odin adjusts

his weight on the knee cushion. "The store I need doesn't open 'til ten anyway, and I wouldn't make it back in time once I got going."

We start to roll through the building and Odin doesn't even stop to look at signs. He must be pretty familiar with this sort of injury treatment. I wonder what else he's hurt through his years of playing elite football. We stop outside a wall of windows, looking in on a huge gym full of machines and padded tables and shirtless men grunting. Muscles flex as they lift themselves and lunge and pedal furiously on exercise bikes. "Wow," I say, totally distracted by the peak physical forms on display in front of us.

"Relax, Janssen," Odin grunts with the effort of opening the door for himself and wheeling through it. I can't believe they don't have one of those buttons to open the door, considering the people coming through it are presumably all injured. Again, I try to help him, and again, he growls and looks pissed off by the gesture.

There doesn't seem to be a waiting room, so I just follow him until we're greeted by a friendly woman in a polo shirt and shorts. "Hey, you must be Odin." She extends a hand, the other holding a clipboard. "I'm Prachi, and I'll be torturing you today." Odin laughs and shakes her hand while my eyes fly wide. I guess black humor is the norm here. Prachi glances at me. "Did you want to hang out in the lounge while Odin works?"

I glance at Odin for guidance, but he just slumps on his scooter, looking forlorn as the pro team's quarterback hops past us on one leg, then the other. I should probably be starstruck, considering sports are a religion here in Pittsburgh. Maybe it's the orgasm hangover, but I feel pretty chill. The only athlete I'm thinking about is the one pouting beside me. He doesn't suggest I stay and watch, though, so I guess I'm heading to the lounge. "Sure. Where is it again?"

Prachi directs me down a hall to the cushiest room I'll ever hang out inside. There are luxurious armchairs, trays of fresh fruit, and a fancy coffeemaker, plus little signs with the Wi-Fi password and bottles of sparkling water in a clear-front fridge. Athletes and their drivers apparently lead different sorts of lives than me, and I try to imagine Fern enjoying this sort of thing with Wyatt once they're settled in the UK. He just signed with a professional soccer team in London, so I'm sure this will be old hat for her soon enough. I text her a selfie from one of the chairs, a bunch of grapes in my hand and a bottle of San Pellegrino tucked under my elbow.

I wish I'd thought to bring my backpack. I don't even have a book with me, which reminds me that I left my copy of *The Redcoat* in Odin's room last night after... after. I'll have to make do with my phone to entertain myself, and I discover that the library has an eBook copy of the sequel to my beloved historical romance by Chloe Petals. I know she lives in Pittsburgh, but I've never had a chance to meet her.

I munch on the grapes and read nearly half the book on the library app before my phone starts ringing in my hand, startling me. It's Odin calling and then texting, telling me to get my ass outside to his car so we can leave.

I grab an apple for him since he's clearly hangry, and smile when I see him leaning against the car, a little sweaty and a lot irritated. "Session go that well?" I tease, unlocking the doors.

He grunts and tosses his scooter in the back. When we're both situated with the radio playing, I start to back out of the parking spot. "Am I taking you home?"

"Where's your errand?"

"Oh," I explain, "You don't want to come along on that one. I'm going clothes shopping."

His brows go up. "You gonna try shit on?"

I flush and nod. Why am I always blushing around this guy? I don't know if I've ever blushed in my life, but something about him makes me feel...vulnerable. Odin grins and rubs his hands along his thighs. "I'm coming with you." I shrug, not sure what to make of this development or even if this sexy, enormous football player would fit inside the dressing room at the thrift shop. I get the car turned toward the Birmingham Bridge so we can cross the Monongahela River. "That reminds me," he says, "I have to tell you something."

"What?" I ask, rolling my eyes. "You want a rematch?"

"No, smart-ass," he retorts, "I just—"

But I don't get to hear what he just did because right at that moment, there's a huge bang, and the car starts swerving like crazy on the bridge with six lanes of traffic.

# CHAPTER 14
# ODIN

"OH MY GOD, oh my god, oh my god," Thora chants as she grips the wheel and slams on the brakes. I hear a chorus of horns wailing around us as cars pass while my G Wagon swerves through traffic.

I clench my jaw, helpless, until she brings us to a stop in the bike lane, the bridge shaking and vibrating under the rush of cars and semis continuing to zoom along its span. "Fuck," I mutter, dragging a hand through my hair.

And then I look over at her, hands over her face, shoulders shaking. "Hey," I squeeze her arm. "You did perfect. We're safe." A car honks, and Thora shrieks, stabbing at the button for the flashers. "Perfect," I repeat, catching my breath. What the hell happened here?

Thora's breathing rapidly in little short puffs and won't make eye contact. She just keeps saying, "I'm so sorry. I'm so fucking sorry. I will make it up to you."

"Hey," I tilt my head to try and find her gaze. "Hey, Thora, I'm not mad." She snaps her eyes to mine, and she looks terrified. I concentrate on keeping my voice level. "This isn't your fault."

She shakes her head. "I will have to pay you back for the damage. I can pick up a few shifts and get you the money after finals and—"

"Hey," I try to rub a thumb along her hand where she's still white-knuckling the steering wheel. Someone put a huge dose of terror into this woman, and I want to strangle whoever made her react this way to what's probably just a flat tire. "Thora, I wouldn't expect you to pay to fix my car, okay? Let's go see what happened?"

She blinks, like she's trying to hold back tears, and I see her throat working as she swallows. "You're not mad?"

"I am not mad. Not even a little bit." And it's true. I'm enjoying myself with her a hell of a lot more than I enjoyed that session of PT, where I learned just how little I'm able to do with my right leg and how the fuck long it will be until I can wear a shoe, let alone walk...let alone run.

Thora whispers, "You're not mad," like it's her new mantra, and I watch her puff out a long, relieved breath before she claps her hands and transforms into a different person—the Thora I'm more familiar with. "Okay, so where's your jack and tire iron?"

She hops out of the car and walks around back before I can maneuver myself out, clinging to the door for balance as I work to keep my bad foot off the pavement. The front passenger tire seems to have exploded, which reminds me that I was supposed to get new tires this spring but kept putting it off because of football practice, and then, well, I thought the car wouldn't be going anywhere. "Shit, Thora, this is my fault. I was supposed to get these babies changed months ago."

Thora squats on the ground near the back seat, grunting as she lifts part of the floor, which I didn't realize was removable. She pulls out the tire iron, dropping it to the ground with a clang. I scratch my chin and reach for my knee roller in the back seat right before Thora flips it up and extracts a jack from beneath it. "How do you know where all this shit is in my car?"

She shrugs. "My uncle works on cars." She starts walking around to the back and flipping open the cover to the spare tire. "Well," she adds. "He probably runs a chop shop."

I flinch. "So, you know how to change a tire, but you were freaking out about doing it?" Cars whiz past us on the bridge, and Thora seems not to notice. She starts lining things up by the passenger side of the car.

"Um," she mutters, "Poor people don't usually drive reliable cars. I know my way around a donut." I notice she doesn't say anything about the freaking out part.

I stare as she works. "At my house, my dad always deals with spare tires." I'm not even sure if we've ever had a flat before, come to think of it, but Thora's mention of not having a lot of money makes sense since I'm pretty certain my parents have always kept up with car maintenance until my dumb ass came along.

"Yes, well, some of us have dads in and out of jail rather than keeping up with inspections." Thora frowns. "I'm not going to be strong enough to loosen the nuts, even if I jump on the tire iron."

"You're not jumping on the tire iron on the Birmingham bridge, Thora." I frown at the situation. Not only can I not play the sport I've spent my entire life dominating, but I also can't even change a fucking tire with my—what is Thora exactly? Anyway, with a woman in the car.

"Don't tell me what to do, Stag." She starts to stomp on the wrench, but it doesn't move. She can't weigh much more than a hundred pounds, and I know she's strong because she hauled the tire over here, but she's not "D1 football player strong." And neither am I—not anymore.

I stare down at my useless foot, resting on a wheeled assistive device. I'm about to pull out my phone and call my parents when Thora says, "I think what we need to do is balance your knee on my leg since I won't roll away, and then you stomp the lever with your good foot."

I blink at her. The idea is fucking weird, and the physics of it sounds wild, but I'd rather give it a try than have to call my mom to come get me when I'm out with a woman I want to see naked. "Hmm," I grumble.

Thora kneels on the ground like she's about to propose and pats her thigh. "Put the boot-knee here. You can hold onto the roof since you're a thousand feet tall." She's right about all of it, and when I finally get myself lined up and take an experimental stomp on the tire iron, we both hoot in celebration as the nut loosens with a screech. "I can't believe that worked." She grins, bending to move the tools to the next nut on the tire.

We work our way around, me grunting with effort and nearly falling, her stoically bearing the pressure of my awkward body, and then I stand by like an asshole while she jacks up my car and changes the rest of the tire. I snap a picture of her with my phone since she looks hot as fuck, with her face streaked with dirt as she tightens a lug nut on a six-figure car.

Which she shouldn't have to do when she's out with me. I realize she wouldn't even be here with me right now if I weren't broken, and I slide my phone back in my shorts pocket without looking at the pic.

A slamming sound shakes me out of my drama, and Thora walks back toward me, wiping her hands on her jeans. "I think I got it on there. Do you want to check the tire before I put the tools back?"

I grimace. "Why would I want to check?"

Her face tightens, and I can tell that she is not only used to people yelling at her, but she also somehow doesn't have confidence that her work is suitable, which means someone probably spent a lot of years screaming at her that she's not good enough.

What's my mom always saying about emotional regulation? Thora clearly didn't grow up with a lot of it around. "Right," she says, tipping her head toward the driver's side. "Well, let's get back in, I guess."

It takes just a few snaps and thumps for Thora to get the car put back together while I climb inside, fishing around the console for hand sanitizer and napkins. I present these to her, and she smiles like I just got her roses, so I decide I should definitely do that later to thank her for putting my car back in working order. "That was incredible," I tell her, turning in my seat and draping an arm behind hers. "You were amazing, you know that?"

She shakes her head. "I was a mess." I swallow a retort because now doesn't seem like the time to dive into her trauma.

"Hey, will you let me buy your outfit or whatever? I owe you big time for changing the tire."

She puffs out a laugh. "You owe me? I probably drove over a piece of glass or something stupid."

"Don't talk that way." I let my voice get stern and realize that's probably not the best way to talk to someone who is obviously upset. "I told you," I say with much more intentional calm. "I was supposed to get new tires, but I kept putting them off, and then I got hurt. This is on me. And no offense, but you'd have to have driven over a long stretch of razor wire to blow performance tires, baby."

"Hey." She snaps her eyes to me as she turns over the engine. "Do not call me baby. I know I'm small, but I am not diminutive."

No, you're fucking not, I think, but what I say is, "Don't pout like one, and I won't call it as I see it, Janssen." She seems to be sliding back into her usual self.

She snorts and turns off the four-ways, easing back onto

the bridge toward Oakland. "Oh," she looks at me. "Where should we go? I guess we have to find a tire place?"

"The Mercedes place is on Baum. Weren't you going to some store on Liberty Ave? We can just do your errand first and drop the car after. I assume you won't go over—what's the speed limit for the spare tire?"

Thora pats my leg. "Now, who's a baby? We'll drive the speed limit and be just fine. But are you sure you don't want to go right to the dealer? I don't want you—"

"We are running your errand, and that's final," I bark. She nods and heads toward the Bloomfield Bridge. If I squint, I can probably find her house from up here, and I consider rolling up there with my brothers and cousins to scream in her father's face and see how he likes it. Between her mentioning prison and her obvious fear that I was going to berate her for a normal flat tire, he seems like he's probably a real piece of shit.

But my time is better spent building Thora up than worrying about someone who is not worth that kind of effort, especially since I can't physically intimidate anyone at the moment.

"I'm buying you an outfit," I say again, impressed as Thora parallel parks along Liberty near a row of shops. I point to a fancy clothing store I've heard my mom mention. "Let's go find you something in there."

She huffs at me, and I ignore her, rolling up to the boutique...where I discover I can't even get in the fucking store because it's got stairs outside.

"Hey," Thora places a warm hand on my arm. "You don't have to buy me anything, Odin. And I'm pretty sure the thrift store has an accessible ramp."

I flip the bird at the bullshit shop and scowl when a store worker sees me, eyes wide through the window. Whatever.

"I better fit inside the dressing room with you," I mutter to

Thora, who laughs and shakes her head. We walk a block to the thrift store that does indeed have a ramp to enter.

"You wish, Stag." But her cheeks flush as she pushes open the door to the crowded shop, waiting for me to wheel inside with her.

# CHAPTER 15
# THORA

ODIN DOES NOT, in fact, fit into the dressing room of the thrift store. It's more of a shower stall, honestly, but Odin barely fits in the store at all. He's just such a huge human being, made bigger with his cast and scooter.

I walk up and down the aisles, searching for "professional research fellow vibe" pieces, and Odin creaks behind me, grumbling that there's no room for him. A dress catches my eye, and I lean past my companion. Spotting the original price tag on the shiny material, I gasp, startling Odin, who furrows his brow. "What?"

"It's new with tags. Oh! And it's my size. I have to try it on immediately." I shoulder past him toward the dressing room, and I hear him following. I wouldn't even know what it meant to find an Alice + Olivia dress in a Pittsburgh second-hand store except for Fern, and I have been daydreaming over an issue of *Vogue* someone left at the bar.

The polo sweater dress has white trim and fancy houndstooth buttons with a really fun spread collar. I'm not even sure what the black fabric is, but the whole thing slides on like it was made with me in mind. I am almost totally flat-chested with no hips to speak of, but as I tug the dress over my head and smooth it along my body, I want to cry because I look amazing. Somehow, this form-fitting dress makes my form look more feminine. I purr as I run my hands along my hips, staring into the tiny mirror in the dim light.

The sound must trigger Odin's impatience because he snaps the curtain open and then freezes when he sees me in the dress. I watch him taking me in, enjoying the obvious lust in his eyes as he stares at me in the $500 dress I'm about to buy for $6.99. His throat works as he swallows before saying, "You're getting that, right?" I nod, smiling. I start to imagine wearing it for him, which is stupid because he's my research partner, whom I fooled around with briefly. There will be no wearing things *for* or with him. Odin grunts. "I have to get out of here. I'll meet you outside in what? Half an hour?"

"Do you need me to go? I can take the car to the dealership as soon as I pay for this—"

He shakes his head. "I told you I'm buying you that outfit. I just need to…" He rubs at the back of his neck and gestures with the fingers gripping his scooter handle. "I don't fit in here." Odin reaches into his pocket, pulls out a wallet, and presses a twenty into my hand. "Half an hour?"

I nod as I watch him go and then work quickly to find a few more new-to-me outfits for my new life abroad. When I'm wearing these things, I don't look like someone whose father orders her to get him a shitty beer.

These are the clothes of a person with regulated emotions and enough of a cushion to approach an emergency with calm. I can't afford these clothes brand new, but I can sneak into them second-hand. I can reuse someone's discard, giving it a second life. I should have given Odin the money back, but something tells me he'd be weird about it, so I splurge a little on a pair of flats that go perfectly with the dress *and* slacks and a boat-neck top I imagine I'll wear while I walk along the Isis river in Oxford.

# CHAPTER 16
## ODIN

I WAS seconds away from coming in my pants after seeing Thora in that dress. It's not even a slutty dress. In fact, it's super professional, which is what she said she wanted. But it clung to her body in ways that set off deeply unprofessional thoughts in my caveman brain.

If she weren't excited about how fancy it is, I would probably take her somewhere and rip it off her. Except I can't do the things I want to do to her because I only have one functional foot. That awareness calms my dick right down, and I wheel down the block toward the bookstore, remembering that I never did get to confess that I ruined Thora's book.

Thankfully, the bookstore has an accessible entrance *and* wide aisles, so I wheel myself inside in search of the romance section. This is where I find my mother...laughing and fiddling with boxes of books along with my Aunt Emma and one of her friends.

I stand there with my mouth hanging open, irrationally wondering if my mom somehow knew what I did to ruin the book I came here to replace.

I eventually realize that's ridiculous and wheel my way over toward her. And she clutches at her chest like she's about to faint. "Odin! You're out and about!" Mom clamps a hand on Aunt Emma's shoulder, and my aunt pats it supportively.

"I do leave the house, Mom. Come on."

She shakes her head. "Of course you do, sweetheart. It's just all those stairs. And you've been so grouchy when Dad and I have tried to call or stop by. Did you find the soup Dad left you?"

"Yeah. Thank you." I stare at the floor for a beat. "I know I've been in a mood. But I've also been leaving the house more."

"Well, what brings you in here? Did you come to help set up for the event?" Mom points at a sign, which informs me that Aunt Emma will be in conversation with Chloe Petals here at the bookstore, talking about the crossover between nonfiction sports books and the historical romance Chloe will soon release about Pittsburgh rowers in the 1800s. Mom, an Olympic gold medalist in rowing, is apparently the host of the event.

"I had no idea any of this was happening," I admit, fidgeting with my scooter, wondering how our entire family is going to fit in this tiny bookstore, let alone members of the public.

Aunt Emma grins. "We've sort of kept this one tight. I know the Stag herd is supportive, but this is more for our rabid fans. Well. Mostly Chloe's rabid fans."

And then the name clicks. Chloe Petals wrote the very book I'm here to replace. Chloe Petals is Mom's friend Chloe, whose real last name is definitely not Petals. I snap my eyes to the smiling woman stacking books by my aunt. I point at her. "You wrote *The Redcoat*."

She laughs. "I sure did. But you're not the demographic I was expecting. You've read it?"

My cheeks heat, which is really saying something because I'm always the guy who has no problem running to the pharmacy for condoms for my football teammates. "I read parts of it. I actually need to replace my friend's copy because I... spilled something on hers."

Chloe beams and turns around, reaching into one of the boxes. "Here you go, kiddo. On the house. Oh! Should I sign it?"

"I don't mind paying for the book."

Mom waves a hand and nudges Chloe with her shoulder. "Yes, sign it and tell the friend Odin's mother wants to meet her."

"You already did," I start to explain, the words out of my mouth before I realize the impact that will have. Mom and Aunt Emma clap their hands and Chloe wiggles around like she hit the lottery. They always act this way when one of my brothers or cousins brings home a date, which is why I don't do that.

"When did I meet her?" Mom taps her chin. "I would remember if my son introduced me to a special someone."

I sigh. "Don't call her a *special someone*, Mom. And you know Thora from the student law clinic, apparently. She's my research partner from class."

"Oooh, Thora," Chloe coos. "That's a great heroine name."

Mom squints at me. "Didn't you say you have a project together in a class? Sweetie, I thought you were doing a medical withdrawal? That paperwork is pretty important for NCAA eligibil—"

"Mom, I got it under control, thanks." I don't mean to snap at her, but everyone is always up in my shit about all of this. To Chloe, I explain, "My friend is Thora, T-H-O-R-A, and she's a huge fan."

Chloe scribbles something in the book and snaps it shut, handing it to me. "In that case, you should bring her to the event. It's sold out, but I happen to still have my two guest tickets to give away."

My brows fly up. Thora will bust an ovary if I bring her to

see her favorite author in real life. I look at the date on the poster—this coming Thursday. We'll be done with our presentation by then. I realize that I've been sort of dreading the end of our time hanging out together, and this is definitely a way to extend that. Maybe she will wear that dress...

"I'd love that, thank you," I blurt as Mom and Aunt Emma exchange glances. It's no use trying to tell them there's nothing particular going on there. Thora is moving to another country in a few months.

She's also the only person in my life right now who didn't know me as Future Pro Football Player Odin Stag. It's refreshing, having her give me shit and fight with me, just for me. And it helps that she's cute as hell. I can already see her sitting ramrod straight in her seat, hanging on Chloe's every word during whatever conversation they're going to have.

I kiss Mom on the cheek, accept an arm squeeze from Aunt Emma, and salute Chloe with the book as I roll out of the store to find Thora, who is just now exiting her store with a huge plastic bag of clothes.

A smile splits my face, and I don't even care about the uneven sidewalk as I make my way toward her. "Listen," I start. "I never got to tell you my confession, but it's all good because I already made up for what I did."

She leans against the brick wall of the thrift shop, seemingly intrigued. "I forgot that you were telling me you did something bad."

"Oh, I'm bad, sugar." I wink at her and hand her the book. She glances down at it, confused. I lower my voice. "I ruined your book last night, but I got you a signed copy as a replacement."

She drops her bag of clothes on the ground and opens the book, chin dropping, eyes popping wide. "It's signed and personalized? Where did you get this??"

I hook a thumb behind me in the direction of the bookstore. "That's not all, though. There's an event here on Thursday."

She rolls her eyes at me like I'm the biggest idiot in Pittsburgh. "Duh. It's been sold out for months. I wanted to go with Fern as a sort of farewell adventure."

My heart sinks, knowing I'm going to offer her both tickets and knowing I won't get to see her in the dress again or spend that time with her. I chalk it up to just one more thing I've lost this spring, but I tell her, "Well, I'm about to make your day, I guess." I pull the tickets from my pocket. "VIP seating and all."

Thora blinks at me, speechless. And then she tackles me into the wall with a hug that sends my scooter flying. Propped on one foot, I lean against the wall as Thora pumps her arms around me like she's giving me the Heimlich. "Thank you, thank you, thank you, you big, sexy hero. How do you have this? Are you made of magic?"

When she finally releases me and sees my scooter all tipped over, me perching like a flamingo to keep my boot off the ground, she starts laughing, and I join her because what else is there to do?

# CHAPTER 17
## THORA

ODIN KEEPS TEXTING me to ask when we can finalize everything for our presentation, and I don't know why I'm avoiding his messages. The man got me tickets to meet my favorite author, and I'm leaving him on read.

It's kind of a lie. I'm avoiding him because I'm starting to think of him as more than just my research partner, and that's the sort of thinking that gets a girl in trouble. Nobody needs to explain to me that I'm balanced on a razor blade. Yes, I've been chosen as a Rhodes Scholar. However, the distance between acceptance and showing up in the United Kingdom is nearly insurmountable. I'm one missed bar shift away from not being able to afford all the details I need to get my ass abroad.

Speaking of, I need to see if someone will switch shifts with me so I can actually attend the event with Fern this week. Odin's face was interesting when he gave me the tickets. Like he didn't really want to hand them over or something. I figured out that his mom is on the panel of speakers, so I'm guessing he's anxious about me spending time with her. I will try to compose myself when I apologize to her about being a dick about this school project in his hospital room when he was coming to terms with his injury.

"Thora!" Fern snaps her fingers in my face across the table at lunch. "I've been talking to you for like five minutes."

"Oh. I'm sorry." I slide my phone under my notebook and fork a bite of soggy quinoa from the healthy station in the cafeteria. "I'm ready now."

She shakes her head and forks her own mushy grains. "I was saying, Friday is my last recitation, and then I'm done. With college. Forever." She beams, actual rays of light shining out of her cheeks.

"It's definitely a weird feeling," I agree, tapping my fingers on my notes for my own math class, where I have definitely not been chosen as the TA like Fern. "It's going to take me a while to shake off the desperation."

"What do you mean?"

I shrug. "We're desperate to get out of here, you and me. Everyone knows it. And it's affected everything about us." She squints, considering, and I lean forward. "I don't own a robe, Fern. That's how little I know how to relax. Do you honestly think we're going to pop off on hikes or watch birds or whatever people do to chill in the U.K.?"

She laughs. "No, but I think we will probably meet up at some soccer matches, right? You'll sit with me to cheer on Wyatt?"

My chest shakes as I try to hold in a laugh. "I've never watched a sporting event in my life, except for what I can see from where I've been working for all of them at the bar or sports arenas." I tap my chin. "Maybe I'll get myself a job tending bar by Wyatt's soccer stadium just to feel normal."

Fern chokes down a final bite of her grain bowl. "I think they call it a football pitch over there. Or something." She pats my hand. "And you won't *need* a job as a bartender. You're going to be financially secure for once."

I nod. "Well, that's what I'm saying. It's going to take adjusting."

We're quiet for a bit until I remember that I haven't told her about the tickets. Her face lights up when I tell her about the bookstore event. "It doesn't go too late," I assure her. "You'll be able to get home in time to get your beauty rest before the final session as, Professor Fern."

"We can sleep when we're old," she says, gesturing for her ticket. "It will be so great to just go do something fun together. We never splurge on this kind of thing."

"Again," I say, tapping the table with my index finger for emphasis. "Adjustment. We are not normal, but we are working on it."

————

I never respond to Odin's texts before the presentation, but I do send him a detailed email and tell him to wear something nice for class on Tuesday. This makes me feel bad because I realize there's no way he can get dress pants on over his cast. At least, I don't think he can. I put on the dress and literally run out of the house Tuesday morning, so nobody can exhale a single puff of smoke on my new favorite material possession.

I arrive outside the class extra early and gasp when I see Odin in a shirt and tie. I had no idea he'd look like...*this* all dressed up, like a bulky GQ model with his broody blue eyes and perfectly styled hair. Even his earrings look classy, and I let my eyes trail down his body, halting when I get to the usual athletic shorts. A laugh explodes out of me, and he joins in.

He grins. "You said to dress nice."

"Oh my god, Odin, you're killing me." He spins in a circle on his scooter, wagging his butt and making me cry with laughter. "I can't believe you put a shirt and jacket on with mesh shorts."

He leans down and puts his mouth an inch from my ear, making me squirm and cling tightly to my bag when he says, "Make up your mind, Janssen. How do you want me?" And then he draws his head back and winks just as Professor Ferda arrives to open the classroom.

"Hey, you two," our instructor says. "Nice and early. Ready to rock?"

———

Odin has his notes typed on index cards. Not just written but typed and printed. I suddenly feel ill-prepared and sloppy next to him, and I never, ever feel that way about schoolwork. Like I told Fern, I worked my entire life toward this 4.0 undergraduate transcript, but I'm about to be shown up by a guy from the football team who, to my best estimate, only started showing up for class once he got hurt. I realize I'm being unfair because from what he's said and what I've seen, the athletes are pulled in a lot of directions, and they're helpless to go against what their coaches say if they want to keep their scholarships.

I zone out, focusing on his lips moving as I stand next to him, fidgeting in my cute shoes and designer dress. I realize the pattern on his tie matches the black and white houndstooth on my dress buttons and know he must have done that on purpose, based on what he remembered of the dress he only saw me in briefly. I know he is starting to think about me as more than a research partner, too, and that scares me even more. There's a reason I've avoided relationships. I can't afford one. Not yet. I still have too much to achieve.

Resigned to cut him off cold after class, I take a deep breath as he cues me up for my portion of the presentation. I adjust my posture, turn my glance toward the class, and perform the hell out of my piece of the argument.

# CHAPTER 18
## ODIN

"THAT WAS AWESOME." My mouth brushes against Thora's hair as I lean in to whisper in her ear. She flushes, my favorite shade of pink splashing across her cheeks in contrast to her dark hair. Why does she do that? I fucking love it, even if I don't understand that response from someone so obviously capable and kick-ass.

Professor Ferda smiles and gives us a thumbs up as the class titters in applause. I realize everyone is probably waiting for my hobbled ass to get back to my seat so the next group can go. I navigate the narrow space between chairs, bumping into shit with my knee roller.

Then I watch as Thora leans forward in her desk, totally paying attention to the next student presentation. I never, ever pay attention to those. I'm not going to start now, but I do watch as my research partner takes notes and focuses. She's probably deconstructing their arguments already and finding weaknesses.

I could walk out of here right now. I'm supposed to go immediately withdraw from school so I can get my medical delay or whatever it's called. I've stopped even bothering to check my email, so I have no idea how many of my other professors are still reaching out. Right on cue, my phone vibrates in my pocket with a message from Meech, demanding that I roll right up to his office as soon as my presentation ends.

I purse my lips and glance at Thora again. I want to do something with her after class rather than fade into her memory as some guy she knew once. She's about to go be a wizard or whatever at her fancy British school. And what will I be? A college drop-out with no career prospects and nothing to do but rehab an injury. It occurs to me that I'll lose my apartment, too, if I leave school. The Stag pad is in a building for student-athletes. Shit. I was going to stay one more semester until my eligibility ran out, and I left for the pros.

So, really, I'm an injured college drop-out who has to move back in with his parents. Yeah, I'm in no rush to deal with this paperwork.

A flutter of applause alerts me to the fact that the group has finished presenting. I watch Thora raise her hand and ask them if they could elaborate on the bias of one of the sources they used, and I laugh on the inside as she arches a brow in response to their inability to answer. She's not flushing now.

Class ends soon after, and I tug on the sleeve of Thora's sexy dress. "Hey." She turns. She's wearing makeup today, just a little. It makes her eyes look huge and her lips really, really good.

I drag a hand down my cheek. "You want to grab lunch? Celebrate being done?" I hope my voice doesn't give away how desperate I am for her to say yes. Because once she says no, that's it. We're not going to the author event together. We're just two people who did a research project for a class she needed to graduate.

Her face falls. "Oh, I can't today. I work."

I will my expression into a grin even though my insides are crumbling. "Well, then, I guess I'm following you for a drink." She smiles at that, and I'm surprised by the amount of relief I feel. "You going to wear that to tend bar?" I gesture at the dress I know she cherishes. I'm so glad she decided to wear it so I can memorize how it looks on her, highlighting every tiny dip in her figure.

Thora shakes her head. "Nah. I was going to change in the bathroom, and Fern was going to come grab the dress and take it to her place. Nobody smokes there…" Thora drops off like she's revealed too much about herself.

"I can take it to my place for you if that's easier. I know Fern takes the bus…"

Thora laughs, a delightful puff of sound. "Yeah, and you take forever on your scooter thing."

I waggle my brows. "Yes, but I have a basket."

———

I roll back to my place after Thora changes in the bathroom, where I tried desperately not to imagine her naked as she peeled off the dress and slipped into her jeans and tank. I ignore a bunch of texts from Meech and my coach. Instead calling one of my brothers to come run the dress up to my room. While I wait, I tear off my shirt, jacket, and tie, glad I wore a T-shirt underneath all that. I stuff everything in the bag Thora gave me, liking that our nice clothes are hanging out together.

Eventually, Gunny stumbles outside like he just woke up, which might be true since the hockey team is finished for the semester.

"Anything else, your majesty?" He eyes the plastic bag suspiciously and starts to open the snap to look inside.

"Mind your business. But can you run me to the Fuel Up? I'm meeting someone."

Gunnar squints and gives the bag a squeeze. "Someone, eh?"

"Can you take me or not?"

He scratches his nuts and yawns but eventually shrugs. "Yeah, let me go get my keys."

———

My brother drops me off without too much hassle, only cursing twice as he watches me struggle to get my knee scooter out of the back seat. "How much longer will you need that thing?"

I look upward, trying to do some quick math. "Two more weeks, I think. Then I get crutches. Or maybe I can walk in the cast? I have to ask."

He grunts. "That fucking sucks, bro."

"Yeah."

He looks at his phone. "I have class for a few hours. Want me to grab you after?"

I nod and slap the roof of his car. "Thanks for the ride."

When I get inside, Thora is pouring beers with both hands, smiling and wiggling her tiny butt to the music blasting. The place is pretty full. I guess a lot of people are celebrating the end of the semester. Next week are finals and then commencement. I tip my chin at a guy who vacates the end stool at the bar for me. I should care more that I'm this level of incapacitated, but I just don't.

While I wait for Thora to serve me, I realize my parents and uncles must be upset that zero Stag kids are getting their degrees this spring, as expected. Wes is playing pro soccer here in Pittsburgh, Wyatt is playing in London, Stellan is taking an extra year for some reason, and me? Well…

"Get you something?" Thora grins and leans her elbows on the bar in front of me. I don't even pretend not to stare at her tits.

"Shot of Glenfiddich?"

Thora rolls her eyes. "This isn't that kind of place, Odin. Best I can do is Johnnie Walker."

I arch a brow. "But does it have a Stag on the label?"

"I could draw one for you if that makes you feel more included."

I laugh and nod. "It would, thanks. I'll wait while you do that."

Thora flicks the tip of my nose and hops on a stool to grab a bottle of scotch from the top shelf. She pours me more than a shot's worth and slides the glass toward me.

"Wish you could do one of these with me." I look at her above the glass, smelling the warm spice of the liquor.

"I can do a shot of soda." She pours herself some from the nozzle into a plastic cup, which she taps against my shot glass. "Cheers, Odin."

"Skol," I say, making her laugh again. She takes an order from someone else, not even telling me what I owe her, which I guess is fine because I plan to sit here as long as she can stand me. I order a burger and another shot before switching to beer. I'm off the painkillers now, and I'm also off my nutrition plan.

My body doesn't know what to do with all the greasy food and alcohol. I can hear my stomach digesting against its will as Thora waits on a few more people, and then the lunch rush dies down, and I'm the only one left in the bar.

"You were great today," I tell her, spinning my empty glass in a puddle of condensation.

"You weren't half bad either, big guy." She gestures at her chest and points at me. "I wasn't expecting you to match your tie to my dress."

I tug on my imaginary cufflinks and glance down at my t-shirt, relieved to notice I have not spilled ketchup on myself. "I can clean up sometimes."

"Yeah, like I said, you only looked *half* bad."

"At least it was my good half." I give my leg a shake.

Thora sighs. "I really am sorry, Odin. I feel like I haven't said that enough. You must be floundering, trying to figure out what's next."

"Ha." I dab at my mouth with a napkin. "There is no next. I'm moving back in with my parents until I become one with their basement couch."

She frowns. "I used to not be able to see a future at all, you know. The first time my dad went to jail when I was in high school, I literally couldn't imagine what life would be like for me. I sort of thought I'd end up working retail or tending bar forever, but I couldn't even see that. I'd think about *after* high school, and it would just be...a black cloud."

"Relatable content." I stifle a burp. I must be well on my way to drunk. Thora doesn't offer me a refill, and I don't ask for one. I focus on my fries.

"But I had a really good mentor in high school. For some reason." She grabs the nozzle thing and a plastic cup and pours me a water without mentioning it. "They helped me apply for college, showed me scholarships, made suggestions. Don't you have someone telling you your options?"

"Oh, everyone's got opinions." I point at her with a French fry. "My uncles want me to go to law school. My dad has told me at least 700 times that I can coach college or pro ball with my playing experience. And let's see...my cousins have offered me free tickets to watch them play professional soccer, as if it wouldn't be fucking devastating to hear Stag this and Stag that while I'm stuck in a cast."

Thora's eyes crinkle around the corners, and her expression is hard to read. "I'm nervous, too, you know? About moving somewhere all alone, the unknown of it all, and the pressure."

I grip the bar with both hands and lean forward until my face is an inch from hers. "You have absolutely nothing to worry about. You're a fucking force, Thora, goddess of thunder." I'm close enough to smell her breath, and I know I'm going to kiss her. I want to grab the back of her head and pull her into me, yank her across the damn bar, and into my lap. She parts her lips, and I know she wants it, too.

But my brother Gunnar's voice slashes the moment. "Yo, Odin, if you want a ride home, I'm leaving now."

I sink back into the stool and turn to face him. He leans against the door to the bar, massive arms crossed over his chest, shit-eating grin on his face. That fucker absolutely timed his outburst to interrupt me kissing my new obsession. I turn back to Thora, who licks her lips and tucks her hair behind her ears. "I'll close out your tab," she whispers, and I nod.

I grab a bunch of cash from my wallet and slide it under my plate. "Have a great time at the book thing with Fern," I tell her.

If she responds, I don't hear her over the squeak of my scooter as my brother helps me out the door.

# CHAPTER 19
## THORA

I TAKE extra time to admire my reflection in one of the outfits I scored at the thrift store with Odin last weekend. While I'm looking at my butt in the mirror over one shoulder, my mom surprises me by tapping on the door and entering my room. "Oh, you look so nice, Thora."

I catch her eye, noting her weary face. "Thank you, Mom. I wasn't expecting to see you today."

She smiles thinly. "It was slow at the diner." She shrugs. "Thought I'd come home for a change." Mom has been working herself ragged. It's not lost on me that she's the sole contributor to the household once I graduate. I'm not exactly sure how my parents will manage once I move overseas. From the looks of my mother, she's not really sure, either.

I smooth my hands down my pants and smile at Mom. "Fern and I are going to a thing at the bookstore tonight. We scored free tickets." I don't tell her they were a gift from Odin or that he looked sad yesterday when he left the bar. Or that he almost kissed me first.

Mom would just tell me that I can't afford to get in trouble with a boy, and I would tell her that I know. I don't need to tell her I have an IUD courtesy of Planned Parenthood or that I'm pretty sure Odin won't be lured into petty drug crimes. Nor will he get sucked into the bottomless whirlpool of poverty if he gets a record and no access to any meaningful employment. I don't need to tell her any of that.

Instead, I kiss her cheek and grab my purse that's bulging at the seams just a little from the signed copy of the replacement *Redcoat* book. I head out to meet Fern at the bookstore.

Once there, Fern is waiting for me on the corner across the street, nervously eyeing the long line around the block of readers eager to get inside. "Wow," I tell her, pulling out my ticket. "I should have thought about getting here early to snag a good seat."

We cross the street, and an employee monitoring the line asks to see our tickets. I hold mine up, and they grin, waving an arm toward the front door. "Ooh, VIPs," they say. "Your seats are reserved right near the front! Enjoy."

Fern's mouth drops open, and I feel the weight of everyone's eyes on us as we bypass the entire line, shouldering our way into the bookstore, where there are as many folding chairs as possible have been squeezed into neat lines between the shelves. There's a small open space up front with a handful of chairs, each with a bright orange VIP sign taped to the back of the seat. Fern squeezes my arm, and we pick two chairs near the back of the special section. I'm really unused to this sort of treatment.

The closest I usually get to a performer is when I'm bringing them drinks before a show. Once, I was tending bar at the arena and I got to take a tray of shots backstage to the band opening for Radiohead.

Now I'm the lucky fangirl with the awesome seats. Soon, every chair in the shop is full, and Juniper Jones picks up the microphone, introducing herself as the host of the panel alongside Emma Stag and Chloe Petals. I wiggle in my seat, whispering to Fern that this is Odin's mom and aunt.

"I know," she hisses back. "They're all related to Wyatt, too, remember?" I swat her arm, secretly overjoyed that she has found such a great guy with a family that loves her as much as I do. I study Odin's mom's face as she talks about the history of rowing in the Allegheny region and her own experience rowing in the Olympics.

No wonder Odin's so obsessed with being a professional athlete if his father played pro hockey and his mother apparently dominated the entire world in rowing. Emma and Chloe start talking about their latest books and I've never been interested in reading nonfiction before now. Chloe Petals is delightful in real life, earnest and open, and I love how she and Emma talk about sharing their research into the sport. Chloe just made it all sexy while Emma—well, Emma made the real-life rowers sound pretty sexy, too, come to think of it.

I clutch Fern's arm as the authors each read aloud from their books, and before I know it, I'm in line to *meet* them. It's a good thing Fern is with me because, for the first time in my life, I'm struck speechless when it's my turn to greet Chloe Petals. Fern pinches my shoulder and greets Emma and Juniper, who peers around the shop and over our shoulders. "I thought Odin was coming tonight," his mother says, brow furrowed.

I shake myself out of my fangirl stupor and tell her, "He gave the tickets to me and Fern. It was so nice of him." I glance down at the book in my hand and then drag my eyes to Chloe's. "Thank you so much for signing my replacement book. Your writing is just—gah! You're my favorite."

She surprises me with a hug, pulling me in tight for a comforting squeeze. "You are so welcome! I always love meeting fans." She smiles at Fern. "Would you two like some photos?"

Emma laughs. "Fern is in plenty of photos with us. We're all going to be in the owner's suite next month when Wyatt starts in the London Derby."

Fern and the Stags start to talk about soccer, and my eyes are on the verge of glazing over when Chloe nudges me. "We have to move through the line, but we can do a selfie, just us if you want?"

I nod and snap a pic, sailing over the moon with the joy of being here, with my best friend, actually talking to authors. I'm suddenly sad to realize that Odin might have imagined being here with me. Was he thinking we'd go on a date?

Fern and I elbow our way out of the crowded shop with waves from the panel, and outside in the night air, Fern sinks against the brick wall of the shop, a smile spreading across her face. "I still can't believe I fell into this family," she coos. Fern never coos. We like each other because we are both practical and realistic.

But here I am, swooning right beside her. Maybe it's because graduation is looming, and things are finally falling into place. A few beats later, she pats my arm. "I teach my final class in the morning, so I better head home."

"Oh." I look at my watch. "Want me to wait for the bus with you?"

She shakes her head. "Wyatt pre-loaded my Uber account." A grin belies her frustrated tone. "I'll be home faster than you, probably."

She glances toward my house, and I nod. She taps around on her phone, and a few moments later, a hybrid vehicle swoops to a stop in front of us. "Catch up soon? We still need to deal with your passport, right?"

I nod and wave as she drives off, and I think again about Odin, sad at the bar. He's got my dress at his apartment. I need to go over there at some point to get it back from him, right? It's barely nine at night on the last week of classes. Surely, I won't be disturbing him if I pop over there now to thank him for the tickets?

The 54 bus chugs up Liberty Avenue before I can second-guess myself, and I hop aboard, heading toward Odin's place. I clutch the gifted book to my chest, realizing he never did tell me what he spilled on the original.

# CHAPTER 20
## ODIN

THERE'S someone at the door. I can hear banging from my bedroom and then my brothers' voices as they greet the visitor. Probably someone from the hockey team come over to play video games with them since I'm holed up in my room moping.

I never withdrew from the semester, which means I will fail all my classes rather than have incomplete grades. Well, I guess I'm getting an A in my arguments class. I'm not sure if I've ever had an A before.

Not that I'm stupid. I've just always prioritized football because that was going to be my career for the next decade. Lotta good that did me.

The voices get rowdy, and I hear Gunny shouting my name. I'm already in bed with the ruined copy of Thora's book, planning to try to read the pages that aren't stuck together. I have no explanation for why I'm spending a beautiful spring evening in bed with a romance novel. I have no explanation for a lot of things these days.

The door opens, and I shove the book under my back. "What the fuck?" I snarl toward the entryway until I see who it is. "What are you doing here?"

Thora shuts the door behind her, a strange smile on her face. "Nice to see you, too, Odie."

"Do *not* call me that. Ever." I sigh and adjust my weight so the book is sort of off to the side. I'm not wearing a shirt and Thora notices. I let her, resisting the urge to flex my pecs as she stares at my chest. "Hi," I say, trying to start again. "I didn't realize it was you. I thought my roommates were just being assholes."

She smiles and drops a bag on my desk, shrugging out of her sweater. Hot damn, she's wearing one of those outfits she bought last week. A sleeveless top thing that nips in at her tiny waist and skinny black pants that leave nothing to the imagination but in a classy way. "Oh, they were being assholes. I'll spare you the details." She starts to tie back her hair. I want to scream at her to stop, to let me run my fingers through it while it's down and dark and all over her shoulders.

But then I think about what she just said. "What did those fuckers say to you?"

I move to sit up, and Thora laughs, shaking her head and sitting on the edge of my bed near my booted foot. "They're harmless. They were just giving you shit via proxy." She smiles at me and licks her lips. I sit up despite her earlier protests before I remember that she will see the book if I move. She points at it. "I came over to thank you for the tickets. And because you never told me what happened to my original copy of the book."

We both stare at the paperback. I'm not sure if she can see the wrinkled pages where the spooge dried, crusty and sticky. "I, uh…" Fuck it. What do I have to be ashamed of? She got herself off thinking about me reading her that book, and it was hot as hell. I look her straight in the eye, and my voice drops, husky and low. "After you left, I was polishing Gungnir and—"

"Gungnir?" Thora wrinkles her nose and raises one brow.

I flash her a full-watt grin. "Yeah. Gungnir. The Spear of Heaven."

"Oh, for fuck's sake, Odin." She swats me with the book, laughing until I yank it from her hand. "What happened to the book?"

"As I was saying! I was polishing Gungnir, and...I got jizz all over the pages."

Thora flushes from her throat to the tips of her ears. I watch the color bloom across her skin as she breathes, as her mouth drops open, and her pupils explode. "Odin." Her voice is an invitation, but the second I think about accepting, I realize there's no way I can perform.

I want to be rough with Thora, dirty. I want to dig my toes into the mattress and rut into her like...well, like a stag. I want to slam her up against the wall, bend her over my desk, and rail her from behind. And I can't do any of it. We stare at each other.

I'm not sure if she figures out what's going on in my head or what, but the next thing I know, she's standing next to me, slowly unzipping her pants and peeling them off her legs. She kicks off her shoes and then climbs back onto the bed, throwing a leg over my hips until she's sitting on top of me, staring as my chest moves up and down like a bellows. "What are you doing?"

She rubs her hands along my skin, and I hiss at the contact. I've been touching myself to thoughts of this for weeks now, telling myself it's okay to fantasize about her because she's leaving anyway. And she knows it because she presses a fingertip into my sternum and says, "This can't lead anywhere, but I really want you, Odin."

"Yeah?" I sound a lot more vulnerable than I want to come across. This is new for me. I don't love it.

Thora laughs. "Of course I want you. Look at you." She runs a palm along my chest, and the other one drops to her collar. "What do you say? Want to have at it 'til I leave town?"

This draws a laugh from deep inside me, shaking off the dreary cloud that's been hanging over my head all day. "Have at it? Did you just say that?"

"Oh, shut up, Odin." And then she's kissing me, leaning forward until her ponytail brushes along my chest. Her lips are soft and puffy, and she tastes sweet, like fruity gum. A moan escapes me as I deepen the kiss, bringing my hands up to her shoulders, to her neck, to her ass, where she sits on top of my growing erection.

"Thora." Her name is like some sort of faucet I open to drain away this darkness, this heavy dread that's followed me since the accident. I moan into her mouth and let my tongue tangle with hers. I wrap her hair around my wrist and tug, bending her head back so I can bite her throat. She likes this, rocking her hips against me when I nip at her skin.

I say her name again, thrusting up against her panties. And then I realize I haven't even really touched her yet, so I let go of her hair and squeeze at her ass. She's firm everywhere, tough like she's had to be, and I pull her down against me, rubbing her along my dick until I can feel her wet heat.

Thora is having her own adventure exploring my chest, digging her short nails into the space between my ribs. She grabs the book and throws it off the bed, and while I have her arms loose, I tug at her shirt up and over her head. "Shit, Thora, no bra?"

Her cheeks heat again, and she bites the corner of her mouth, shrugging. "I don't really need one…"

She starts to cover her breasts with her forearm, and I snarl, batting her hand out of the way and sitting up fully so I can tip her back in my lap and suck her nipples. Just as I hoped, I can fit almost her entire boob in my mouth, and I move between them, sucking and biting as she wriggles around and hangs onto my shoulders. We haven't even taken off each other's underwear, and this is already the hottest sexual encounter I've had…maybe ever.

This absolute beast of a woman shoves me backward with a shriek and starts crawling backward down my legs, tugging at the waist of my shorts and briefs in one handful. I raise my hips to help her out and close my eyes, so I don't have to see her struggle when she gets to my cast. If that happens, I don't notice because the next thing I know, Thora's mouth meets the head of my cock, and I practically black out.

# CHAPTER 21
## THORA

ODIN STAG IS ENORMOUS. His entire body is proportional, and the dick I find inside his athletic shorts is hard and proud, pulsing and weeping precum from the uncut tip. I cannot help myself. I have to taste it.

And so, I do, lowering my head and sticking out my tongue to meet his hot skin as he hisses out a curse. I glance up to meet his eye as I slide him into my mouth as far as I can, and his expression might just ruin me forever. Odin is awed right now. There's no other way to describe the look he gives me as his hand gently drops to my hair, his fingers brushing along my cheek as I start to suck. I know my cheeks are hollowed out, and I almost feel my gag reflex kick in as he shudders involuntarily with what I assume is intense pleasure.

My name slips out of his lips, his deep voice practically purring. "Oh, fuck, Thora, that's incredible. Look how fucking sexy you look with me inside your mouth." He groans, his fingers in my hair tugging, a tingle along my scalp. I wrap one hand around the base of his cock and let the other explore his balls, warm and heavy in my hand.

As I bob my head up and down his length, I hear him slapping the mattress, and when I look at him again, he has the side of one hand crammed in his mouth, biting back a roar. Curious, I let my finger explore behind his sack, sneaking between his taut cheeks. I find the tight pucker of his ass and tap it, causing Odin to growl. I swear he flies into the air like a falcon.

I don't know how, but he turns and flips us both, so I'm on my back with my legs around his neck. "You want to make me cum before I fuck this pussy, Thora? Is that what you wanted?" Odin drags a finger along my panties, which are soaked to the point of ruin by now. He shoves them to the side, and my breath hitches as he slides one massive finger inside me. "Oh, this *is* a greedy pussy. You want the Spear of Heaven, Thora? Is that it?"

I laugh at his joke, but when I meet his eye again, I see he's dead serious. "We aren't joking about pussy. Not tonight." And then his face is between my legs, and his teeth are on my clit, and I forget to breathe as he wreaks havoc on my nerve endings.

"Odin. Holy shit. Wow." My hands scramble around the sheets, looking for something to grab as I feel the slow build of pleasure I almost never get from a partner. "It's so good," I whimper. He continues to lick, adding a finger inside me, pumping as he works my clit from the outside with his tongue.

"Do you always shave your pussy bare, Thora? Or is that just for me?"

I can't speak. I'm too worked up to answer him, but then he stops all his movement and begins lowering my legs. "What are you doing?" I try to sit up, and he gives me a side-eye.

"I'm taking off these fucking panties, so I have more room to work."

"Oh." My breath returns along with some semblance of

thought. "You don't have to keep going. I can't really come that way. Remember how—"

"Thora." He puts one hand under my chin and looks right into my eyes, probably all the way into the back of my brain. "Do I look like I'm fucking bored?"

I glance down to where his other hand is stroking his massive erection, which…might be even harder than it was when I had my mouth around it. "Do you *like* doing that?"

He arches one brow. "Eating your pussy? Fuck yeah, I like it. I've been dreaming of doing that for weeks." He pulls open the drawer next to his bed. "Lie back."

I hear a familiar buzz and look over to see the blue cock ring I used when I got myself off alone here in the bed as he read to me from the chair. I now have a Pavlovian response to the sound and sight of it as Odin presses it against my upper thigh. "I said lie back, Thora." And Thor help me, I do as he commands.

I sink into the bed. My legs tipped open wide as he starts licking and stroking me again, now with the vibrating toy added into the mix. He teases me with it, holding it every-where but my clit, but somehow the combination of his tongue, his fingers, the toy, and the knowledge that this is sexy to him…uncorks whatever usually holds back my plea-sure during these sorts of encounters.

"Odin," I gasp, my hands flying involuntarily to my nipples, needing just that last bit of stimulation as the dam breaks and the pulsing, joyful white heat of pleasure bursts in my center, sparking through my limbs and back again. I must be screaming. I must be a mess. But I cannot find the energy to care, and then Odin's mouth is on mine again. I can taste myself on him, and I've never experienced that before, either.

When I open my eyes, he's smiling at me, an expression I know is dangerous for what this has to be: two people fucking around before graduation. A final, shuddering sigh slips out of my lips against his before he asks, "Can you keep going? Do you want me inside you?"

I should tell him no. I should get dressed and leave. I should delete his number from my phone before anything else happens that would potentially jeopardize me leaving this country. Instead, I reach for the drawer, where he has a strip of condoms, and I pull one from the row and tear it open. "Lie back," I echo, repeating his instructions earlier and figuring this will go easier on his injury if I'm on top.

He does as I say and watches as I roll the condom onto his dick. He feels so warm and stiff under my hand. I cannot wait to feel him stretching me open. I swing a leg over his hips and am about to impale myself on his delicious cock when he places a hand on my thigh. "Hang on." He flicks on the toy, grinning as he rolls that down his length. "Oh shit." His body trembles and shakes as he grows used to the sensation. "That's…wow. Fuck, Thora."

I grin, keeping his gaze as I slide onto him. We both moan as we press together, and I relish the feeling of fullness, the stretch as he opens me with his body. And then the toy is buzzing between us, pressing into him and into my clit at the same time. His mouth falls open, and there is that facial expression again, the one I cannot allow myself to return as I grip his shoulders and roll my hips. I ride Odin Stag as he chants my name, as his hands dig into my hips and pull me closer, offering me more and more friction. A second passes, or maybe it's an hour, but we're both coming. He swells impossibly large inside me, grunting and pulsing as my body jerks and spasms, the second orgasm hitting me much harder and longer like the first was just some warm-up act for the most explosive pleasure of my entire life.

When it ends, we stare at one another, terrified. Silently, Odin reaches for the toy to shut off the vibration, and as he slides out of my body, I nearly sob at the loss of him. I know he's right here beneath me, but I also know I cannot keep him and allow myself to want to.

"Odin," I whisper, shaking my head. "I can't."

He runs his fingers through the mess of my hair and nods. "I know." And he closes his eyes, rolling to the side to sit up and deal with the condom. He doesn't ask me to stay over, and I don't.

# CHAPTER 22
# THORA

I TRY to rush out of my parents' stinky house as soon as I wake up. The last thing I need is to catch whiffs of stale cigarette smoke while I'm trying to take a math exam. But as I dart through the kitchen, I spy my mother at the cluttered table, drinking coffee.

She offers me a watery smile, and I can tell she's been crying.

I purse my lips and open the back door, letting a gust of warm air into the kitchen as I sink into the seat opposite her and pat her hand. "Hey, Mom."

She blinks a few times and smiles. "Hey, baby." She doesn't add anything further, but I look down at the table. Between her hands, I see the red stamp of an overdue bill. My heart sinks, sensing bad news.

I tilt my head toward the paper. "Is that the electric?"

Mom shakes her head. "This one's from the piss tests."

"Oh." As part of my father's house arrest, he has to submit urine pretty regularly to verify he's not using, and each time it's at his expense, which is Mom's expense since he's not working, although he could be. I try to collect my thoughts and remember my research mission. He's not working because the jobs available to him are grueling, menial, and low-paying.

But also, he's just adding to my mother's burden, and that pisses me off. "How much is it?"

A tear rolls down Mom's face, and she reaches for my hand. "I'm not going to be able to take off next Sunday for Commencement." She waves a hand at the paper. "It's this or the rent, and we're behind on that, too."

———

Fern keeps staring at me from our seats on the bus as we head downtown in search of our student visa paperwork. She taught her final math recitation this morning, and I aced a final exam despite being up all night long. Now, we're hitting our checklists hard. Passports, visas, and bank accounts we can access from the United Kingdom without spending a zillion dollars on fees.

Fern pokes me in the nose at a red light, causing me to yelp. "What the hell is wrong with you?"

She squints and leans close to my face. "I was just checking to make sure you're alive." She snaps her fingers in front of my face.

"Will you knock that shit off? Fern. Stop it."

My best friend harrumphs but backs out of my physical space as much as she can on a crowded bus where I'm squashed against the window next to her. She hums. "What happened last night after the bookstore?"

I shrug. "Nothing," I lie. "I slept in my bed, in my parents' stinky house, and got up in time to make my mom breakfast for once." All truths there, the last part. It was good to see Mom for a bit, sipping coffee in the quiet before she dropped the bombshell on me

Fern shakes her head. "Something is going on. You know how it works, Thora. We tell each other our crap, and then we figure out a plan to solve or endure the problem."

I stare out the window, debating which news to break first: that I slept with Odin, and it was way more intense than it had any right to be...or that my mother revealed she can't come to my commencement. I turn to face my best friend and talk around the knot choking me from the inside. "I have to give my airfare money to my mom if I want her to be able to go to Commencement next weekend."

Fern's face falls. I know she's about to offer me money or tell me that her mom will take pictures and video or some workaround, but the truth is I really need to feel sad about this. "Don't tell me anything that will make it better, okay? Not yet."

She nods and drapes an arm around my shoulders. "That really, really sucks, Thora."

I rest my head on her, enjoying the familiar, soft weight of my person—of the friend who knows what it's like to sit on the edge of something better and feel the constant threat of it all being yanked away. I want *someone* to prioritize me, and it's not ever going to be my family, and the sooner I accept that the sooner I'll stop feeling this way when shit goes wrong.

My phone buzzes in my lap—a text from Odin. I wince before I read it, I'm not ready for any more emotional bombs to drop today. But it's pretty benign.

ODIN STAG

You get home okay?

I send him a thumbs up and turn to face Fern. "What would you do?"

She's quiet for a few blocks as the bus bounces over construction dips along Fifth Avenue. Hardly anyone gets on the bus on this stretch of road between the universities and the downtown office buildings. "I think I'd give my mom the money and get myself a slutty tank top to work some doubles at the bar."

I snort. "Two grand is a lot of double shifts."

She hums again and tugs on my arm, pulling me down the aisle and into the City-County Building and the passport office. We're waiting in line when she snaps her fingers. "You said two grand…was that for a round-trip ticket?"

I blink at her. "Well, yeah. I need to come back."

She shakes her head. "Not for an entire year. What if you just bought a one-way and figured out the rest once you're over there." She taps on the paperwork in her hand. "Maybe there will be a discount sale or something. I don't know."

I don't say anything as I consider her suggestion. She already has her phone out, searching for flights and I peer over her shoulder, feeling a lot less hopeless when I see the prices for one-way tickets. There is even a direct flight from Pittsburgh to London that I could work off the cost if I get picked to work at one of the country music concert venues this summer. I squeeze my friend and kiss her on the cheek. "That's a terrific idea, Fern Montgomery. Thank you."

I'm not sure if it's my improved outlook or our extreme preparedness, but the passport and visa applications are a breeze. That includes getting fingerprinted and having our retinas burned into the computer system—or whatever they did with our eyeball scans.

Fern suggests we take the train to her apartment for lunch, and soon, I'm nestled into her couch with peanut butter banana sandwiches and reruns of *Gilmore Girls* on the television. "I'm going to miss you," I tell her after a big swig of milk. "What if nobody over there understands me?"

She laughs. "They probably won't understand either of us. Between the Pittsburgh accent and our lack of refinement…" I stifle a burp and laugh. And then all my feelings settle in alongside the heavy peanut butter in my belly. "Seriously, though," she says, "You'll be an hour away. We won't have part-time jobs in grad school, you know. For one thing, we won't have work permits…"

That draws a laugh from me, but I suppose she's right. I will *only* be working on academic labor for the first time ever. Part of my brain immediately tells me I can always seek out under-the-table work in a pub. I entertain brief fantasies about sending money home to my mom so my parents can maybe cover their expenses without me.

I shake that away and quietly fantasize about walking over the Tower Bridge arm in arm with Fern, both of us in yellow raincoats. Because that's what I imagine people wear in London.

Fern takes my plate from me, sets it on the coffee table, and turns to face me, arms crossed. "Something else is up with you, though. What happened?"

I purse my lips. I guess it does no good to avoid telling her I slept with Odin since she's basically married to his cousin. I stare at the ceiling and blurt, "I went to the Stag apartment last night after you got on the bus."

When I look at her again, her eyes are wide and wild, and she's grinning like a weirdo. "How was it?"

I roll my eyes. "You know it was great."

"Seriously? It's never great for you with someone."

I grab a throw pillow and clutch it against my middle. "Yeah, well, I guess these guys know what they're doing in that department."

Fern flops back against the couch next to me again. "They really do. Or Wyatt does…"

"I told you he was the one to give your flower to."

She whacks my arm. "I told you to stop calling it my flower." We watch Rory and Lorelai Gilmore try and fail to prepare frozen pizza until Fern adds, "But if it was so good, why do you feel glum?"

"Because I like him. There. I said it." I sigh. "He's funny, and he gives me shit in a good way, and, well, he knows how to make me come, and now I'm leaving the freaking country."

"So?"

"What do you mean so? This is exactly the worst time to get involved with someone, Fern. I should be focused on my future. I need to work double shifts so my mom can watch me be the first person in my family to get a diploma. I don't have time for romance."

"Hmm." We're quiet again as the Gilmore gals have a similar discussion on the television. Fern points at the screen. "It's just that...so what if the timing sucks? Why not have a fling and enjoy yourself before you go?"

I consider this because I've been considering it since I left Odin's blue gaze late last night and felt the sting between my legs with each step I took today, reminding me of how he worked with me to find a way to make my body sing.

He wrote back at some point, reminding me he still has my dress and to let him know when I want to grab it from him. I should respond. I should say something about him wanting a booty call...keep things light. I should take Fern's advice and ignore my emotional connection to him while enjoying the pleasure sensations he knows how to strum up.

Fern continues, saying, "Enjoy it while it lasts. And maybe he'll visit Wyatt in London, and you can have a vacation booty call this fall."

Maybe she's right, and I can keep things light with Odin. Perhaps we can keep playing card games for sexual stakes, and if he gets a different cast, he can take me tubing in a river and make me come on a rock in the woods like a forest fairy. Or maybe all of that is a fantasy because nothing is easy like that. Not for people like me.

When the episode ends, I hug my friend. "I gotta go," I tell her, standing and stretching. I'm working close tonight at the bar."

"Slutty tank top," she says, clicking off the television and walking our plates toward the sink. "Make lots of tips, friend."

She blows me a kiss as I back out the door to her apartment and make my way to work.

# CHAPTER 23
# ODIN

MOM

Have dinner with your father and me...

I LEAVE Mom's text unread all day Friday while my cousin drives me to and from physical therapy. I also leave it unread while I shower for the first time without a boot on my leg. I mean...obviously, I don't take my phone in the shower. But the whole thing is a huge process I really shouldn't have tackled alone, and I'm not sure why I don't respond to my mom or call on any of my roommate-relatives to help me out.

Instead, I bite back moans of pain as I balance my ass on the tile and scrub my itchy-ass leg. I try not to look at the scar and bruising at the incision. I try not to think about what Thora might think if she saw me now, hobbled like an injured bird trying to scour lint from between my toes.

Thora.

Our night together was incredibly intense, and I know it scared her. She couldn't get out of here fast enough afterward. I don't know what the hell to do about her. She's leaving at the end of the summer. I know that. And yet, she's the best thing in my world right now.

I can't believe I went into that encounter thinking it would be terrible, I couldn't perform the way I usually do, do the things I typically do with women. Nothing about Thora is usual or typical.

I have no idea where she got the idea to play with my ass while she had my dick in her mouth, but I was a nanosecond away from exploding down her throat before I used some sort of ninja maneuver to flip us both over, cast be damned.

Post shower, once I have my cast back on, I'm about to face the music and read my mom's text, but the phone rings instead, and it's my dad. "Gah," I say by way of greeting.

"Never ignore your mother, Odin. It worries her, and then she pesters *me* about it." His tone is pretty neutral, so maybe this won't be as painful as I feared. No lectures. No litany of questions about my future.

"I was about to text her back," I tell him, grunting as I tug a pair of shorts up and over the cast. It's a new boot with some wedge in the heel, but I'm still only allowed to take it off to shower, and I've got two more weeks with the damn scooter.

"Yes, well, you waited too long. I'll be at the apartment in five minutes. I'll be double-parked, so start heading outside now." I don't have time to react to this news before he adds, "Are you good on the stairs yet? Should I park?"

I debate my response for too long because Dad hums, and I know he will park and offer to carry me. I am tall and coordinated enough to monkey-swing my way down the stairwell with my arms pressed to either wall, but I still need someone to carry my scooter down. I haven't yet gotten to the point where I want to throw it down the stairs and hope for the best.

By the time I get a shirt on and find my deodorant in Gunnar's bathroom—he's always stealing my shit, and I'm not going to miss that when I move out—Dad is in the doorway giving the apartment a condescending scowl. "Dad," I say, nodding my head in his direction. I roll over to him as he lets his face melt into a more familiar grin, and he opens his huge arms to wrap me in a hug. Honestly, I do feel better once I'm all wrapped up in a Tyrion Stag embrace. He's always been a good hugger.

"Lead the way, O-man. What should I do?" I demonstrate my hands-on-the-wall-and-swing-down-the-stairs technique, and he follows it with my knee roller. He blocked a hydrant with his ancient gold minivan, so I do my best to hurry into the passenger seat as if anyone would give hockey star Ty Stag a parking ticket. The man can, and has successfully, grinned his way out of everything.

Dad drives me to the house, pulling into the garage he recently redid and pointing at the ramp that has replaced the step into the kitchen. "You never know," he explains. "Seemed like a good idea. You know, in case your mother becomes infirm."

She hears this joke as we enter the house and whips him with a dish towel before pulling my face down so she can kiss my cheeks and ruffle my hair. "You had me so worried, Odin Theodore. Don't do that again." Holding me at arm's length, still awkwardly bent down, Mom studies my eyes like she's trying to look inside my head. "Go on and sit. I brought out the ottoman for you to rest your cast."

I don't bother to ask what inspired this private meal. I've been ignoring absolutely everyone but Thora, so I'm sure Mom has a notepad of prioritized to-do items to get my life back on track. The problem is, I don't think the tracks have been built yet. Or someone lost the blueprints. Or something.

Dad produces a huge takeout bag full of Mediterranean food, and my mouth waters at the smell of the hummus, feta, and fresh parsley. As predicted, Mom pulls out a yellow legal pad.

"I'm just going to dive in if that's okay," she says, not referencing the food but assuming full-on lawyer/judge mode. I nod because there's no stopping her once she starts questioning a witness. "I took the liberty of calling Brian. You remember your cousins' agent? He was Uncle Hawk's agent, too—"

"I know who Brian is, Mom."

She nods and takes a bite of cucumber. "Well, I told him you aren't pursuing representation any time soon." I silently swallow a mouth full of falafel and watch her cross AGENT off her list with a swift, precise pen stroke. "Now, you'll need to sign some paperwork from your coach, whom I've convinced to hold off pestering you for another week while you sort things out with academics. But anyway…"

I stop listening as Mom reiterates that my scholarship requires me to stay on the roster for the team during my rehab. She talks about minimum grade point average and academic eligibility and ten thousand things I already knew. I tune her out and bury my fingers in my hair, tugging it to feel the sensation on my scalp.

My life has exploded, and I can't even wallow. I have to do paperwork about it. When I open my eyes again, Dad has his hand pressed reassuringly over Mom's pen, and they're both staring at me.

"Hey," Dad says. "Tell me something good that happened this week." Mom nods and presses her lips together, setting the pen on the table.

I take a sip of my water and tell them about my presentation with Thora. "I think we aced it. Did I tell you she's a Rhodes Scholar?"

Dad's brows lift, and he nods, impressed. Mom grins. "This is the girl from the law clinic, right? She was so nice at the reading, although I thought you were coming along with her, sweetheart. I hope you didn't stay home because of your leg. I could have—" Dad squeezes her shoulder, and Mom stops rambling.

I take a deep breath. "Thora wanted to go with Fern." I hold my palms up. "I wanted them to have a nice night out."

Mom hums appreciatively. "Fern leaves soon. After Commencement, right? I think Wyatt is flying home to support her. Isn't that so sweet?"

Dad nods. "Very sweet, June-bug."

We all eat quietly until Dad grabs the notepad and scans the list Mom scrawled down an entire page. He looks at me and folds his hands together on top of the list. "What's one thing you can take care of this week, O?" He holds up a thick finger. "One thing."

I scratch my chin. I haven't shaved, but somehow, I suspect personal hygiene is not what Dad is talking about. I'm pretty sure I missed the window for the medical withdrawal, and I can't stomach being in the football building right now. Not with the team all high on success, working out next year's roster, and preparing for their own futures with the game. I'm sure the paperwork with Coach is important, but that feels as far off as going for a jog.

I think about Thora and what it means to her to finish a degree at all costs, let alone graduate school afterward. She mentioned how hard her mom has to work to support the three of them without a degree. My family is in a different place, financially, but it sort of feels like spitting in Thora's face to piss away the credits I've earned so far. I rap my knuckles on the table and look at Dad. "I'll call Meech and deal with my grades this semester. Maybe I'm not failing everything."

Both my parents smile. Mom reaches for her pen to cross something off the list, but Dad shakes his head and squeezes her hand. He looks me in the eye and says, "One step at a time, kid."

He's right, of course. My entire life has been derailed to

the point where a shower takes me longer than it used to take me to run a 5k. Mom and Dad have ideas about what I should do—that much is obvious—but I have to figure out the next steps on my own. I'm not sure they understand that my even wanting to do that decision-making is a huge step up from last week. If it were up to Mom, I'd already have a new strategic plan for my life with goals, sub-goals, and a timeline.

Instead, I tell them I'm proud of getting my dirty dishes to the sink when I finish my pita. Everything is different now, and I know I can't stay in the apartment if I'm not an enrolled student. I know I can't stay on the football team if I can't play football anymore. I know all of that. But moving home isn't something I can handle right now, either.

Dad shoves an entire falafel ball in his mouth and swallows it, turning to me. "Come on, kiddo. I'll take you back to the Stag Lair."

I roll my eyes. He and my uncles have been trying to name our apartment ever since Wes and Wyatt first moved in. I hoist myself up onto my scooter just as Mom shouts that we can't forget more condoms for the safe and satisfied basket.

# CHAPTER 24
# ODIN

TURNS OUT, Meech was more than happy to talk to me on a weekend. I texted him about meeting up on Monday morning, but he called me the second my message went through and told me he was en route to my apartment—something about *his* boss getting in trouble if too many college athletes fail out of school.

I don't feel ready to make any decisions about the fall semester. It was going to be my final one, and I was probably going to graduate in December with a degree in psychology, even though I never really cared about psychology. It just had classes that fit the best around practice and weight training. Next winter, I was going to head to the pro football combine and enter the draft.

I explain to Meech that I'm fine with having a low C average for the semester. The A I'm looking at in my arguments class is holding everything together. He arranges for me to take an incomplete for a few classes until I can handle the final assignments sometime this summer. I can stay in the apartment—for now.

I don't have to leave the apartment except for physical therapy. For now.

It feels like a starting place.

———

I fall asleep Saturday night, wondering what Thora would think of my progress, which means I wake up Sunday confused about why I care what my class research partner thinks. It's not like she's reached out since we slept together. She's leaving the country. We were both just celebrating a job well done.

But I still have her dress.

Gunnar says he'll take me to the dry cleaner on the way to family dinner today, which feels like a fair trade. I hadn't planned on going, but my brother reminded me that Aunt Alice does amazing things with sweet potatoes and chicken. She's used to cooking for elite athletes, and it's not every day we get to indulge in a delicious feast that meets all of our restrictions.

Not that I have restrictions anymore.

Gunny squeezes his black BMW X5 onto Uncle Tim's street, lined with other black SUVs, signaling that we're the last to arrive. I aim my knee roller toward the front door, but Gunny shakes his head. "Aunt Alice said to come in around back this time."

I shrug and wait for my brother to open the fence, where I can see that the backyard is sliced in half by a new wooden ramp leading up onto the deck. I groan, realizing they must all be talking about me and my condition. I don't even want to know how this ramp got here, but I guess it's pretty cool that I can get into a place easily for once.

I roll into the kitchen through the sliding door and see Dad, Uncle Tim, Uncle Thatcher, and Uncle Hawk deep in conversation over a map of the neighborhood. They look like they've just gotten back from a run, all sweaty in matching Pittsburgh Forge shirts courtesy of Uncle Hawk.

Not going to lie; it's pretty cool that they are all still out there being active, even if they bitch and moan about their creaking joints. Dad has them all doing "yoga for mid-life," and there's talk of them hiring a private instructor for all the Stag men and their wives.

Gunnar scoops Aunt Alice up from behind and kisses her cheek as she swats at him. "Gunnar Stag, I've told you to stop lifting me in the air."

He steals a cube of chicken from the pan she's stirring on the stove. "But you're pocket-sized, Aunt Alice. I can't help it."

She swats him with her spoon. "And tell your brothers to stop picking at the potatoes. I set out nuts and pickles for appetizers."

My twin brothers, Alder and Tucker, holler from another room that they have finished the nuts. Then, some more of my cousins start cracking jokes about nuts and pickles until my mother whistles and tells them all to stop being buttheads.

I do love my family. This whole crew is loud, crass, and ridiculous, but everyone is on the same side, and that's the Stag side. I think back to when my cousin Wes's girlfriend ran into trouble with some creep from Soccer USA. The family all jumped in to make sure she and Wes had what they needed to sue that fucker and keep him away from athletes forever. It was the same when my cousin Wyatt had issues with his creepy bio dad.

Speaking of Wyatt, who is currently in London with his new pro soccer team, I'm a little surprised to see his girl-friend, Fern, here at Stag family dinner. I grab a cup of water and roll towards her, where she's deep in concentration with Aunt Lucy. "Hey," I say, scratching my chin. "Wasn't expecting you today."

Aunt Lucy shakes a finger at me. "Excuse me, sir, that is no way to talk to Fern. Of course, she's at family dinner. She's family now." Lucy squeezes Fern in a side hug, which Fern seems to find delightful.

Fern smiles up at me. "Hey, thank you again for the tickets to the book event the other day. It was awesome." And then she makes a face that tells me she knows exactly what happened afterward between Thora and me.

I clear my throat. "I'm glad you guys had fun."

Aunt Lucy furrows her brow. "Book event?" She locates my Aunt Emma across the room and hollers, "Emma Stag, have you been having literary festivities without us again?" The crowd goes silent while everyone tries to decide if they should be pissed off that my aunt would dare do any publicity without including twenty-plus members of the family.

Aunt Alice cuts the tension by announcing that dinner is served, and everyone forgets any potential slight in the rush for first dibs at the meal. I roll to my place between my brothers and shove my knee scooter out of the way once I'm seated.

Since Wyatt's abroad, Fern takes his usual chair across from me, and I ask her if she's ready for graduation next weekend.

Fern sighs dreamily. "Is it cheesy if I say I was born ready? Obviously, it's been a lot of work to get here, but I keep pinching myself because it's finally happening."

She forks a bite of food, and Aunt Lucy tips a ton of wine into Fern's glass, but Fern's smile fades a bit. I frown and ask, "What's with the face? Something wrong?"

She waves a hand. "Oh, no, Lucy pouring my drink reminded me that Thora's at work today."

The sound of her name sends my heart racing a little faster, and blood rushes to my groin. The other night was definitely not a "get it out of my system" situation. Or my system still has a lot more Thora Janssen in it. I clear my throat. "Isn't she always at work?"

Fern bites her lip and leans closer, voice low. "She's really doubling up, though. Ugh, she'd kill me for telling you this, but she had to give her airfare money to her mom for the rent so that Mrs. Janssen could be there for commencement next week."

I pause, letting that sentence sink in fully. "You're saying Thora is paying her family's rent?"

Fern nods. "They had some unexpected expenses. Thora's really upset. Ugh, don't tell her I told you." She sighs. "She's so close, Odin. It's hard to see the finish line getting bumped further away."

I nod, eating quietly while my mind races. I look around the table and glance out the back window at the row of six-figure cars that could finance Thora's life a million times over. Hell, last month's royalty check from the video game with my avatar could buy Thora upgraded airfare. Now she's working double shifts to pay her family's rent?

———

After lunch, I find my Uncle Tim in the kitchen rinsing dishes and loading the dishwasher, muttering to himself about noisy, nosy siblings. "Hey, Unc. Can I ask you something?"

He turns, looking delighted to be asked for advice rather than help scraping food from plates. "Sure thing, Odin. How's the leg feeling?"

"Meh. Pretty numb still." I tap on the cast. "It's not about that, though. I was wondering...how you'd go about giving money to someone who doesn't want to take money."

He smiles. "This is an excellent question. What sort of money are we talking?"

I throw one hand in the air. "Hardly any. Like a thousand bucks. Maybe two if I can finagle it."

He nods and squints over my shoulder toward his youngest brother. "Your Uncle Hawk has a foundation...

would the...recipient perhaps be a woman in need of legal support?"

I purse my lips, considering. "She's trying to get to Oxford to study international family law policies. I want to pay for her airfare. I don't want to take money from Uncle Hawk's foundation."

Uncle Tim grins and rests a hand on my shoulder. "Ah, but we could funnel your gifted money *through* the foundation...we just need to convince her to accept it, right?" I nod. "Let's create a surprise micro grant program she can be selected for!"

I shake my head. "That sounds too easy."

He asks me what sorts of things the "recipient" is involved with at school, and I draw a blank until I stare at Fern and remember something Thora did a few months ago to help Wyatt. "She volunteers at the student law clinic on campus and helps people get free legal aid," I say. "She knows Mom from her guest lectures there."

Uncle Tim rubs his palms together. "Sounds like she's about to be chosen for a distinguished service award, doesn't it?"

He tells me to give him a few days to sort out the particulars and to create a way to hide my donation. I feel energized and excited for something, and I honestly never thought I'd feel this way again. It's like I won a game, and the game is getting Thora what she wants and needs. None of it makes any sense, but damn if it doesn't motivate me to be more of a human and less of a couch cushion.

# CHAPTER 25
# THORA

ODIN STAG

What are you up to?

I STARE at his text in between customers at the shitty hot dog stand in the baseball stadium. Why's he texting me? Okay, I know he's texting me about sex.

It has to be that, right?

It was good sex. He probably wants to have some more of it. He's such a dreamboat, and I can hardly believe this fling is real.

I'd definitely rather be doing Odin Stag than pulling hot dogs from boiling water at a food stand with no tips. When Mom said she could get us a last-minute gig during the day today, I thought she'd at least have us at a bar cart. Nobody tips the hot dog girl.

I pluck a dog from the water with a pair of tongs and snap a selfie, sending it back to Odin.

He sends me back a GIF of an old man squinting through a magnifying glass.

ME

Yes, Stag. Your wiener was also hard to see with the naked eye.

ODIN STAG

That is no way to talk about Gungnir. Are you naked with those tongs right now?

He's funny today. I like it.

ME

Working the Black Sox game and then closing shift at the bar.

ODIN STAG

Don't you have finals tomorrow?

ME

Yes, Mom. What of it?

He doesn't need to explain to me that I'm burning the candle at both ends. It's nothing my mother hasn't done before. If she can pull doubles for weeks on end, I can handle it for a week until I finish my exams. Then I can probably almost get eight hours of sleep per day while I save up the rest of what I need to get my ass to England.

I ignore my phone for the rest of the ballgame, which ends at the top of the ninth because the Sox are losing like usual. Mom and I part ways, her taking a bus home and me heading into Oakland to work the closing shift at Fuel Up.

When I glance at my phone again, I see another text from Odin:

You're acting like me, Janssen. Get some rest.

———

Tuesday and Wednesday bring more of the same, except I'm getting fewer messages from Odin during the day, and I need to remember to see my advisor one last time before the end of the week. I'm feeling pretty good about my performance on my last few exams, considering my legs and lower back throb constantly now, and I'm running entirely on coffee and anxiety.

I figure, these baseball players are knocking out games three days in a row. That has to be at least as much work as scooping up fries and nachos in the same amount of time. I'm basically a pro athlete, but my sport is food service.

I'm starting to feel the impact by the time it gets dark on Wednesday, though, and I'm messing up drink orders. I drop an entire pint of dark beer when I look up and see Odin sitting at the bar along with two of his roommates.

"Hey, now," Gunnar says, reaching around the tap for the glass I dropped. There's still an inch of beer left in the bottom, and he swallows it quickly with a wink in my direction. Odin looks at him with murder shooting from his eyelashes.

"Sorry, boys. I wasn't expecting to see you." I don't even have to force a smile; seeing them lifts my whole mood. "What are you having?" I tap my chin and squint at them, all lined up on bar stools. I know Gunnar and Odin are brothers, and Stellan is their cousin, but they really do all look very similar. The Stag genes must be potent.

That's an extremely delirious thought to be having right now, and if I needed further proof that I'm working too hard, I forget their drink orders the second they're done speaking. "Sorry." I pull out a notepad, something I never need unless it's swamped and we're serving food. "Tell me one more time?"

Odin frowns as his cousins order lite beers. "Just a lemonade, I think," he says, and they tease him. Truthfully, I don't know if I've ever served just a lemonade at the bar. Most people who aren't drinking alcohol get a soda or a mocktail. I first slide Odin's unusual drink and work on the foamy beers for his entourage.

Gunnar slides me a credit card and asks me to start a tab. I eavesdrop while he and Stellan ask Odin about his progress in rehab for his leg.

I immediately feel bad that I haven't asked him more questions or any questions since the first day I drove him there, when we changed the tire.

He talks about doing his regular upper body workout under supervision, as well as one-legged deadlifts and things on his good leg. "And then," he says sadly, "I'm almost up to spelling out the alphabet with the toes on my right foot. You know, real taxing shit athletes do."

Gunnar winces and wraps a thick arm around his brother while I wipe off the bar, trying not to look like I'm listening to every word. "I'm really sorry, brother. You know that, right? We all hate this for you."

Odin grunts and stares at the television, where pro hockey game replays dominate the four screens along the back wall. Soon, all three of them are watching in silence and I busy myself serving other customers. No wonder Odin was eager to work on our project in person and hang out afterward. He's really working through an identity shift from god among us to…a dude who has to work hard on ankle circles.

I can't dwell on this too long because a big table orders tater tots and vodka sodas. A wave of tiredness hits me as I'm waiting for the tots to come out of the fryer, and I almost cut myself slicing the limes for the drinks. I rally and arrange the drinks on the tray just as the bell rings for the appetizers. Happy I can bring it all out together. I turn around to grab the food from the service window and bring it to the kitchen. I guess I turn too quickly, though, because I'm lightheaded as I step behind the bar.

I'm not fully aware of tripping, but I do notice the wet slosh of the drinks hitting my shirt and the hot burn of the tot oil on my throat. The pain passes quickly as I am enveloped in strong arms, the smell of cottony laundry detergent and spicy deodorant.

# CHAPTER 26
# ODIN

THE SECOND we walked into the bar, I knew something was up with Thora. Initially, I resisted going out with my brother and cousin, but now I am glad I have help as I watch Thora trip and fall with a tray full of glass.

I skid across the floor, not sure what happens with my cast, and scoop her into my arms as she hits the ground. She's all wet with spilled alcohol, and some people scream at the commotion, but I don't think she's cut anywhere.

When I glance up, my brother has hopped behind the bar like he works here or something, shouting how Gunnar Stag, hockey star, is here to treat everyone to a guest performance. I would laugh at his foolish behavior if I weren't so worried about the woman in my arms.

"Odin?" Thora struggles to get out of my lap, but I hold her tight. There's no way I'm letting her go back to the grind. Who knows how many hours she's already been working. Judging by the dark circles under her eyes, she hasn't slept since the last time I saw her, and that's been days.

I realize we are physically close for the first time since we slept together. Well. We didn't sleep, did we? We also didn't fuck. That was some next-level connection, and it rattled both of us. We can talk about it later, though. Right now, Thora needs a shower and a long sleep with nobody disturbing her.

Stellan sets my knee roller beside me. "I'll get the car," he says, turning immediately toward the door. Thora stops wriggling in my lap, and someone—maybe the manager? Comes around from the back and asks if she's all right.

"No," I shout at the same time she tries to insist she's fine. I growl. "She's exhausted. I'm taking her home to rest."

The woman puts her hands on her hips and glances around the crowded space. Midway through finals week and, the place is bumping. I know Thora will be pissed at losing the opportunity for tips tonight, but she can't be pushing herself until her body collapses and still plan to finish with the 4.0 grade point average she insists she needs.

Gunnar slaps the bar to get the manager's attention. "Hey, I'll be taking over for Thora there," he says, winking. I swear, every woman in the place swoons. What a clown. I'm grateful.

Thora has accepted that I'm holding her and rests her head against my chest. Her boss crouches down and asks, "Does he know what he's doing back there?"

I shake my head, and Thora shrugs. I glance up, and he appears to be pouring a beer to applause. The manager sighs. "Okay, well, get some rest. This is weird, but people seem to be into him."

I debate explaining hockey culture to Thora's bar manager, but if she doesn't understand by now, nothing I can say will help. Thora and I struggle to our feet. I grip my scooter with one hand, keep the other firmly around her shoulders, and guide her toward the door just as my cousin pulls up outside.

I don't know if Thora is just that exhausted or what, but she falls asleep against me in the back seat of Stellan's Jeep.

It's only a few blocks to the apartment, just enough time for me to text my Uncle Tim that he needs to finalize the grant ASAP. I tell him it's an emergency, and he immediately responds that the plan is to give her the award at some ceremony Saturday night before commencement.

I glance at the woman in my arms and delete the message thread. I don't want her to catch a glimpse of anything and get suspicious.

Stelly turns around to look at me after he parks. "Want me to carry her?" I shoot him a death glare, and he holds up his palms. "Hey, man, I'm just an extension of you here. You know I have a boyfriend, right?"

I blow out a breath. He's right. I want to be the one to carry Thora upstairs, and six months from now, I could be. But the truth is I can still barely get myself to my bed. I nod, and my cousin comes around to the back seat to get my goddess of thunder.

"Since when do you have a boyfriend?" I follow along behind him, dragging my scooter and eventually leaving it at the bottom of the stairwell. Someone will bring it up to me and I can hop to my room once he gets Thora situated.

"It's new," he grunts, kicking open our door and striding into my room. He sets Thora gently on the bed, and she sighs and wakes up.

"Hey," I whisper. "You're at my place. I can sleep on the couch if you want, but you're staying over."

She opens an eye, and it glares at me, making me laugh. "Don't tell me what to do, Stag."

"Don't pass out from exhaustion at work, Janssen." I sit on the side of the bed, waiting to see what she says next.

She groans and rolls onto her back. "It's weird to just accept help."

"Get used to it, Toots. I'm helping."

She rolls her eyes. "Looked like it was your cousin helping, actually." And then she winces, recognizing that that was a low blow. I lie back next to her, and she rolls to her side. "I'm getting booze all over your sheets. I stink."

"There's been worse in my bed. At least it's not barf?"

She swats me, but there's no heart in her effort. She closes her eyes again. "I'm always the one cleaning up the mess. I don't know how to be the one someone cleans up."

I roll on my side to face her as I hear the unmistakable sound of my knee roller hitting my bedroom door. I owe Stelly big time for this. "Hey," I tell Thora. "Even with a jacked-up leg, I'm taking care of you tonight. Deal with it."

She bites her lip. "Why, though?"

I risk touching her face, letting a finger trace down her cheek. "I don't know. You got under my skin, I guess. I have nothing else to do."

That draws a laugh from her, and noticing that her shirt really is kind of gross from the spilled drinks, I hoist myself out of bed and hop over to my dresser. I pull out the smallest shirt I can find, make my way to the bathroom, and grab a wet washcloth.

When I get back next to her, she's half asleep again, and I start to peel off the soaked shirt. "I'm not getting frisky, honest," I whisper. She grunts. I get the shirt up and over her head and absolutely do not register that she, once again, is not wearing a bra…in public. I dab at her beautiful skin with the damp cloth, watching as goosebumps pebble her chest and arms. "Hold tight," I tell her, sliding the shirt over her head. It goes to her knees, which is good because I peel her jeans off next and get her tucked under the covers.

I open my bedroom door and toss her clothes in the hall, then text our apartment group chat, asking someone to run them through the wash before morning.

I flick off the light and am about to make my way out of there to the couch when her arm shoots from the bed and grips my wrist. "Stay," she says, a command and a plea all at once.

Even in the dark, I can see the need in her face, the hesi-tancy, and the fear about what it all means. She's leaving; that won't change anything, but we can be friends. I promised I'd take care of her broken body and all. I curl up against her in my bed, tuck her close against my side, and fall asleep with Thora Janssen in my arms.

# CHAPTER 27
## THORA

I WAKE UP IN A PANIC, not sure where I am. And then I realize the hot coils wrapped around me are Odin's massive arms, and … I still sort of panic. But it feels different. I'm curled on my side, facing him, and I can make out the smooth features of his face in the dim morning light that sneaks around his curtains.

He's here because I asked him to stay last night. I remember tripping at the bar, him freaking out, and then I just succumbed to exhaustion once I realized Odin Stag wasn't taking no for an answer. Nobody has ever growled like that in defense of my health. God, his brother even took over my bartending shift. That could have gone really great or incredibly awful. I wonder if I'm fired.

Just as the financial panic about that sets in, Odin stirs, sees where he is, and pulls me even closer to him. "You're not sneaking away this time." His low voice vibrates through his chest. I love the rumble of it. His body is just so safe and strong and available to me right now. It's all very confusing and not something I'd like to allow myself to crave since it's all very temporary.

But maybe it's okay if I indulge for the day. Perhaps it's okay to let him hold me while I drift back to sleep, just for a minute.

———

I wake up again to a gentle shake and open my eyes to see Odin's blue ones in the bright light of full morning. At least I hope it's not later than morning. I sit up. "What time is it?"

He grins. "Not even eight yet. But I, uh, need your help with something."

I smooth my hair with my fingers, realizing I'm wearing a huge shirt Odin must have put on me last night. The cotton is soft and worn and smells like his detergent. I'd steal it if my parents' house didn't reek of smoke. "What do you need? I definitely owe you."

He shakes his head. "You don't owe me anything. But I'd love it if you could help me with this." He gestures at his cast. "I need to work on showering, and doing it at home is a benchmark for me." He drifts off, staring at the bathroom.

I watch his throat work as he swallows and then turns back toward me, brows lifted in a hopeful expression. I'm touched that he's making himself vulnerable for me after I was sort of forced to be vulnerable last night. Maybe we're a better match than I initially assumed. Okay, we definitely are. I rest a palm on his considerable thigh. "What can I do?"

He grins. "Mostly make sure I don't fall on my ass. I have a chair I'm supposed to use. I can take the cast off in the bathroom, but I still can't put any weight on my foot at all."

I nod and stand, facing the small bathroom. "It's going to be crowded in there."

"Think you can handle the press, Thora? I can get Gunny to help if you're overwhelmed."

I laugh. "I can handle a tight fit."

I expect him to make a joke about that, but he wheels his scooter into the bathroom and turns on the shower, setting out his towel on the counter. He starts to strip before I prepare myself, and there, in the bright overhead light, is the firm ass of Odin Stag. I can't help myself. I am powerless to resist laying a hand on it. It's right there in front of me.

"Don't push me," he says, then bends to remove the cast. I swallow, reminding myself that we are being vulnerable together. He didn't invite me in there to fuck in the steam. I'm not supposed to think about his skin all warm and soft from the hot water. He groans in pain, and my thoughts sharpen immediately.

I step closer as he places his palm on the tile wall, peeling off the boot cast with a creak of plastic hinges. I try not to look down at his heel, where I know his incision must still be pretty gross. He breathes out heavily through his nose, meeting my eyes as he pivots into the shower and sinks onto the chair.

Odin rests his head on the wall of the shower, letting the water fall over him. I can tell he's hurting but doesn't want to say anything about it. I strip off his shirt and step into the shower, putting shampoo in my palms and walking toward him.

His eyes fly open when my fingers dig into his hair, but then they drift closed again as his face eases. "That feels so good," he moans.

"Shh," I soothe, finishing his hair and reaching for his washcloth and the bar of soap. "Does it count against your therapy goals if someone else washes you off?"

He shakes his head. "My instructions were to safely enter and exit the shower independently."

"You did great. Where do I sign?" I urge him to lean forward, and he rests his cheek against my stomach as I scrub his back. His hands are still white knuckling the arms of the shower chair, and I'm not sure what hurts him specifically, but he seems to enjoy what I'm doing, so I continue.

"When do you have to be somewhere today? I can have my brother drop you off…" He sucks in a breath and twitches when I scrub his armpit.

"Ah, ticklish. Noted." I move the washcloth around to his chest. He leans back again, and his eyes are half closed, not staring at my tits, though one of his hands does find my butt cheek and gives it a squeeze. Tit for tat, I suppose. "I have one exam, and then I have my final meeting with my advisor to make sure everything is all set for graduation."

"Ung." He turns his torso, stretching or reaching for something, and I notice a pair of tattoos on his shoulder blades.

I touch them with a soaped-up hand, tracing the outline of a stag leaping over laurel branches. "Tell me about your ink."

He smiles. "All the Stags have that one." He points at his shoulder. "It's tradition."

"And the other one?" I move to scrub that side of his back, where a blackbird perches on a Viking helmet.

"It's dumb," he says and shrugs. "You know, Odin. Viking shit."

I smile. "Hi. My name is Thora. I don't think it's dumb."

Odin grunts and spreads his legs on the shower chair. I can't tell if he's half hard or if his penis is just like that all the time. When I was up close and personal with it, the thing was massive.

"I, um, think you should do your lower half," I tell him, and he opens his eyes, nodding. I back out of the shower and grab myself a towel from the cupboard where I saw him grab his earlier. "When does Wyatt get into town? I know he's accompanying Fern to London on Monday…"

"He's here," Odin says, leaning forward to wash one of his feet. I had never noticed his feet before, but they look strong. I like the tendons and calluses I can see. He moves to his injured leg and washes a bit more gingerly, blowing out another breath before explaining that Wyatt flew in late last night, but he's at his parents' house since they picked him up at the airport.

"He probably went to get Fern immediately," I say, patting my hair dry and looking around the room. "I, um, don't have any clothes but the fucked-up ones from last night."

Odin snaps off the water in the shower. "We washed those for you," he says. "Give me a minute, and I'll grab them."

And then he grips the chair handles, nostrils flaring as he concentrates on lifting himself using just one leg. I reach out to steady him, but he shakes his head. "I'm up." He hops a few times toward his bed, dripping water.

I laugh. "Let me at least wrap the towel around you before you soak everything in sight."

It's strange to be naked with him like this, blotting him dry before he eases himself back into the cast. There's nothing sexual about what we're doing, but it's intimate. Maybe more intimate than anything I've ever done. We're both aware of it as he tugs on a pair of mesh shorts and wheels himself from the room, returning soon after with my shirt and jeans from last night.

I step into the pants commando as Odin watches, shocked. I shrug. "I can do a test and a meeting with no undies. I'll change when I get home."

"Fuck, Thora." He drags a hand through his hair. "You're going to give me a stroke."

"That's what she said." We both laugh as I gather my things and leave, promising to touch base before I go to work in the evening.

———

My legal studies exam is a piece of cake, and I finish early enough that I can walk to my advisor's office at a leisurely pace. There's not a pre-law major here at the university, but between the political science classes and my work in the student law clinic, I feel good about my prospects after my fellowship year. Everything is so close I can taste it, and I shiver in anticipation as I gently knock on my advisor's door.

"Come on in, Thora," Mark says, his voice cheerful.

I wave and take a seat opposite his desk. "Just here for the final checklist for Sunday."

He chuckles. "Let's not get ahead of ourselves. There's still Saturday to deal with."

I furrow my brow. "Saturday?"

He looks at me over the folder he's studying. "Yes, the diploma ceremony. Surely you received the invitation?"

I nod. "I did, but I just thought it was optional. I didn't take off work Saturday." The night before commencement is one of the busiest nights of the year at Fuel Up. Not only will it be jammed with graduating students, but their alumni parents will also be in town, craving the nostalgia that comes with cheap, well-drinks. They always tip really well, those alumni parents.

Mark shifts uncomfortably in his seat, tugging at the collar of his shirt. "Thora, I, um, would really like you to consider attending. You're a Rhodes scholar. We'll be acknowledging that in the more intimate setting of just students from your major and—"

I shake my head. "I still don't have the funds I need to buy my plane ticket to BE a Rhodes scholar. I have to work on Saturday."

Mark gives his collar another yank and leans forward. "End-of-semester awards are granted at the ceremony, Thora. Let's say…you have a strong chance of receiving some funding." His eyes dart between his computer monitor and my face.

I frown. "I can't miss a guaranteed lucrative shift for a strong chance, sir. I'm really sorry."

Mark groans and pinches the bridge of his nose. "I'm

pleading with you to attend," he says. "I'd like to offer my personal assurance that you will not regret it."

————

I leave his office deeply confused. I applied for every grant I could find, every bit of funding. Fern and I spent spring break last year making lists. If there was a scholarship, I'd be aware of it. Something feels off.

# CHAPTER 28
# ODIN

MY MOM INSISTS on driving me to PT on Friday, which is sort of weird since she usually has court on Fridays. When I open the apartment door, she bounces on her toes a bit and looks excited. "It's all set, babe! We did it."

I arch a brow at her as I lock the door behind me. "What did we do?"

She swats my shoulder. "The scholarship! Your Uncle Tim worked it all out with the women's law foundation, and Thora will receive the award tomorrow night at her diploma ceremony." Mom wraps her arms around me and squeezes. "Want to be my date?"

"You're going?" This feels risky. If we show up at her event on Saturday, Thora will absolutely know my family is involved.

Mom nods. "I was always going. I was a guest lecturer at the student law group a few times this year. I'm giving a little talk. And now I'm giving a new award! I saw her resume, honey, and this award should have existed anyway. Dad and I are very proud of you for wanting to help, but keep the spotlight off yourself for doing so."

Mom talks about the importance of this kind of last-mile

award as she carries my scooter down the stairs. I've perfected my monkey swing and we're in the car in minutes. Unfortunately, she invites herself to watch my entire session, but Mom takes an academic interest in this sort of thing since she has a background in elite rowing.

She even asks the therapist if rowing is a reasonable expectation for me for cardio. Mom knows about adaptive rowing machines that don't use the leg muscles at all, and I tune out while the two of them talk about my expanded workout potential. I can watch Thora receive this money. I can see her face when she realizes she doesn't have to worry about her plane ticket.

Mom drops me at home, promising to pick me up early tomorrow and take me to dinner before the ceremony. I wish we could bring Thora with us, but I realize there's absolutely no way to swing that without setting off her alarm bells. Instead, I text her a thank you for making sure my janky ass didn't slip in the shower like a senior citizen.

———

On Saturday afternoon, I cram myself into my business on top best with the most respectable shorts I can find to pull over my cast. I search for my cufflinks, remembering that they're in the top drawer of my desk where I hid the video game royalty check.

I look at the now-empty envelope, crumple it up, and toss it in the hall so someone can recycle it later. The whole scene makes me wish Wyatt were here, which is why I think I'm hallucinating when I hear his voice from the hall. "Littering now, O?"

I don't fight the grin that splits my face. I open my arms and my cousin steps in for a hug. Well, as close as he can get around my roller. He pats my shoulder. "I came to check in on you. Mom said you've been conniving."

His voice and expression are pleasant. That's unusual for him. "Um, yeah. Hey, man, you sound weird."

"It's called endorphins. I feel them now." He laughs. Then he stops laughing. "I feel bad bringing that up. Sorry."

"Nah. It's okay." I tug at my lapels and raise my brows at him. "Do I look okay for a smarty pants diploma thing?"

He laughs.

I return to my cufflinks and he reaches in to help. I watch his thick fingers struggle as much as mine, and ask, "Do you think Thora will hate this? The scholarship?"

Wyatt groans. "I think she will hate it if she knows you're involved. She and Fern...they have this whole thing about handouts. You got any food?"

He doesn't wait for my answer, but walks to the kitchen and returns a minute later crunching raw carrots. I say a quick prayer of thanks that I can at least eat proper snacks now that I'm not in training anymore.

I continue our analysis session, arguing, "It's not a handout, though. She should have this money."

"Mm-hmm." He swallows and gestures at me with a carrot. "I agree. I tossed some more money at Dad's foundation. They have a whole track now that funds the future lawyers, not just the legal funds for the women who need help. You did a good thing, dude."

"Thanks, man. That was cool of you to throw some of your millions back at the foundation. You look...happy. Beyond the endorphins, I mean."

"Speaking of," he swallows again. "I'm down to just one individual session a week with the team psych. Even got the green light to miss a session while I'm here fetching Fern." He grins.

"Is that a good thing?"

"Yeah. It means I'm dealing with my shit." Wyatt sits on my bed with the carrots. "The team there has a whole staff for mental health. There's a dedicated person who works with the injured guys."

That gives me pause. I look at him in the mirror over my shoulder as I smooth out my hair. "That's someone's whole job? Talking to injured athletes?"

"It's their whole ass job."

I want to ask him more about this, but I hear the door and the sound of Mom greeting Gunnar. Wyatt hops up to hug her and tells me he has to get going to Fern's award thing. I follow him into the living room, telling him to call me before he leaves town. Mom rolls her eyes when she sees me and pats my knee. "At least you wore a dress shoe."

I shake my foot. "And a dress sock. This is one of Dad's, I think." It's tall and yellow with tiny hockey sticks embroidered all over the material. She laughs, and we make our way to the car and onward to the ceremony.

We arrive at the law building, and Mom makes small talk with some of the professors, who acknowledge me the same way they did when I was ten. Like some kid who doesn't really belong in this room. Which is true. There's nothing for me here except Thora.

She walks in alone, wearing one of the outfits she got when we were at that store. Once again, it looks like it was custom-made for her. I slip away from Mom and roll toward my brilliant girl. Wait. Okay, fuck it. She's brilliant, and for the next month or so, she can be mine. We're at least friends. "Hey," I tell her, and her eyes shoot upward, widening in surprise.

"What are you doing here? Did you set this up?"

Thora's eyes dart around the room, and she fidgets with her purse.

"Did I set up a graduation ceremony for smart kids? No." I laugh to try and set her at ease. "I'm here with my mom. She apparently has been a guest lecturer for you guys."

Thora nods, and I watch her shoulders relax a bit. She

bites her lip. "I called off work to be here. They were already mad at me about leaving halfway through Wednesday night..."

"Did Gunny not serve as a suitable replacement?"

That makes her laugh and I feel accomplished for a minute until someone in a suit bangs a spoon on a water glass and calls everyone to pay attention. "Good evening, scholars and families," the suit guy says. "If you could all please find a seat, we'll get started. I know we all have a busy day tomorrow!"

Some of the undergrads cheer and hug their families. Thora sits on the end of a row, alone. I try not to take it personally that she didn't sit with me. I did tell her I'm here as my mom's date. I zone out while they talk about how hard everyone worked for four years, how smart they all are, and how important political science is to society. I perk up when they start listing international fellowship awards and call Thora's name as a Rhodes scholar. I whoop loudly. Mom smacks me, but Thora turns and smiles at me, so I don't care.

Then, they call Mom to the mic. She gives one of her typical speeches about how she grew up in the foster care system and relied on scholarships and need-based aid to get through college and law school. She discusses the importance of family law to her judicial career and pivots to the women's law foundation and the work they do supporting their clients.

"And that's what really brings me here," Mom says. "I have one last surprise award for a student who has volunteered countless hours in the law clinic on campus and who has helped others achieve the small legal victories they needed in order to achieve big things in their personal lives. It's my pleasure to award a five-thousand-dollar grant to..." Mom points at Thora. "Thora Janssen!"

Thora turns white and stands with her hands over her mouth. I tug on my ear to make sure I heard correctly, but half the room is repeating the phrase "five thousand," and I have no idea what is going on. I promised like twelve hundred bucks to my uncle's foundation for the award, thinking I'd cover her plane ticket since that's what she was worried about.

Thora makes her way to the stage and takes the check, shaking hands as people take her photo. Mom wraps an arm around her and smiles, then slips away while other bigwigs from the college congratulate Thora.

"Mom," I hiss. "Five G?"

She waves a hand. "Oh, please. She needed way more than you donated, and once some of the other law firms heard about her, they all chipped in. This seemed like a nice number to get her from here to there, don't you think?"

————

When I finally get Thora alone at the punch bowl, she's still rather white and shaky. "You gonna make it?"

I hand her a glass of the sweet liquid. Usually, I'm not able to drink something with this much sugar, but I'm still enjoying a no-restrictions diet, so I clink my plastic cup against hers as she stares at me. "Ooh, this is gross." I set my glass down on the catering tray in the corner.

Thora shakes her head. "Did you know about this?"

I sigh. "Thora. I had no idea you were getting five thousand dollars today," I tell her in all honesty. "But I loved watching your face when you did." I bump her shoulder. "You don't have to worry about shit now. You can just...fly off into the sunset."

She nods and continues sipping the punch she obviously finds acceptable. "I've never experienced not worrying. I don't know what to do with myself."

I grin. "I can think of a few ideas if you're stuck." I wink at her, and she shoves me, so I pretend to lose my balance and roll back in my scooter, causing her face to twist in alarm. "Just fucking with you."

"You are terrible," she digs a finger into my shoulder. "And those socks are atrocious."

"You love it. Come to my place and watch me take them off."

She sighs and shakes her head, setting her empty punch cup on the tray by my full one. "Nah. I gotta go get ready to graduate tomorrow. Isn't that wild?" She looks at the check sticking out of the pocket of her purse. "And I guess I need to stop by an ATM to deposit this."

I clutch my heart. "Thora. Do you mean to tell me you don't have mobile banking? There's an app for that, sweetheart."

She rolls her eyes. "Bye, Odin. See you around."

She turns to leave. "Call me," I beg, shooting my shot. "Let me take you out."

She looks down at the check and back up at me, and I watch as she spends an eternity deciding what to say next. "Yeah, okay," she says. "That would be fun."

I try not to jump or pump my fist in victory as she leaves the ceremony.

# CHAPTER 29
## THORA

MOM SQUEEZES my hand on the bus as we ride toward the arena along with 10,000 other folks, all graduating today. "We're probably the only ones taking the bus to the ceremony," she says, smoothing her hair.

"First of all, definitely not. Second, we don't have to fight anyone for parking! We're way ahead of the game." Nothing is going to get me down today except maybe the thought of Fern leaving tomorrow. Neither of us has really taken the time to absorb the fact that we'll be separated for the first time in four years.

From the day I met her at first-year orientation, she's been my person—someone who understands my background and struggles and can really feel the magnitude of my successes when I have them. And today is definitely a success.

Mom dabs at her eyes with a crumpled tissue. "Nobody I know ever graduated from anything," she tells me.

"I know, Mom. But you set me up to do it." And it's true. My mother showed me the importance of hard work and perseverance every day of her life. Even if I don't understand what she gets from being with my dad, I still absorbed her ability to roll up her sleeves and get shit done. "And I'm going to work on changing things. You know, so other families have it easier."

She squeezes my leg and then stares at it. "Shouldn't you have one of those robes or something? For graduating? You did in high school..."

I laugh. "Fern has our gowns." I don't add that she kept them at her place so mine wouldn't stink. "We rented them." The bus stops at the bottom of the hill, and Mom and I join the herd of families huffing and puffing their way up DeSoto Street. The mood is joyful, like when we're working on game day and the home team is favored to win. Only I'm not working today. It's my show.

I'm still not over winning that award last night. I haven't told anyone. A small twinge of guilt pricks at my side, knowing I should tell my parents, but I won't because if they ask me for some of the money, I know I won't be able to tell them no. The second the money showed up as a pending deposit in my account, I bought a plane ticket and ordered a laptop. I don't want anyone to change their mind about the award.

I spy Fern at the bottom of the stairs, flanked by her mom and Wyatt. She starts jumping and waving, her blue gown billowing in the breeze. I hurry on ahead and clutch her hands, jumping with her in a circle as she tries to stuff the gown over my head. Wyatt clears his throat and hands us each a mortarboard and tassel.

I realize my mom hasn't met Fern's mom, Heather, or Wyatt, so I quickly introduce them. And then there's nothing left to do but line up while our families take their seats. Fern and I are oddly quiet as we listen to the band warming up before we march in.

"Hey," I whisper, squeezing her hand. We're supposed to organize by major, but with this many thousand people, nobody is taking roll or saying anything beyond the posters taped to the walls as an attempt to organize.

She turns to me, a dreamy smile on her face. I lick my lips, and she fishes a lip balm from a pocket somewhere. "Thanks. Also, I won a grant last night." Her eyes widen, and her mouth drops open. "Five thousand," I whisper.

She punches my shoulder. "Shut up. What for?" I explain how it was some legal aid reward for a student volunteer. "I don't remember anyone winning it last year, and it wasn't something I could apply for, so it really feels too good to be true, honestly."

"Hmm," she nods. "Any strings attached?"

I shake my head. "And it was a check to me, not the institution. I cashed it last night and bought my ticket *and* a functional computer. Oh, shit. I had it sent to your house, and you'll be gone." A tuba blares, and then the band starts "Pomp and Circumstance."

Fern leans her head on my shoulder. "You can still send stuff to my house. Mom will be happy to see you when you come pick it up."

We process into the arena and all the families pack the seats, cheering and waving. Fern somehow spots Wyatt and waves, face brightening. I'm shocked by a twinge of…something that Odin isn't there. Why would he be? I push down that unidentifiable feeling and focus on finding our seats and listening to the speaker tell us our lives are about to get awesome.

By the time the Chancellor tells us to stand and turn our tassels, I'm sort of numb and floating. Today is the day. I have reached the finish line. I'm a college graduate, and nobody can take that from me. Ever.

In a daze, Fern and I make our way back outside, eventually finding our moms and her man candy. They're very lovey, making out like fiends as Heather raises her eyebrows and tries to look at me and Mom.

"Well," Heather says. "Should we try to find lunch somewhere that's not mobbed?"

Mom presses her lips together. I didn't lay out any expectations beyond the ceremony. It hadn't occurred to me that, of course, regular families go out to eat or otherwise celebrate occasions like this. You'd think after years working in food service, that would be upfront in my thoughts. Mom stammers. "I, um…" She turns to me. "Sweetie, I have to get home to your dad, and then I have an afternoon shift. You know how it is with the fees."

I nod and hug her. "I know, Mom. I'm good."

Fern and Wyatt stop sucking face to wave goodbye to my mother, and the Montgomery crew invites me to Wyatt's favorite hole-in-the-wall deli for a sandwich, at least. "My treat," he says. And I accept only because he offered to run back inside and return my gown and Fern's to the rental collection.

"He's a keeper," Heather says, and Fern nods.

Lunch is all about England, how Fern leaves in the morning, and how she's going to make notes on everything I need to know and understand before I get there. At one point, Wyatt raises his water glass toward me and says, "Congrats on the award, by the way. Well earned, I'm sure."

And while I know Fern might have whispered it to him when I wasn't looking, I still don't quite understand how Wyatt knew I won an award. He must see my face contort, though, because he says, "Aunt Juniper leaked the news last night." He shrugs. "Stag family gossip. Sorry."

Fern squeezes his shoulder. "They all sent a video congratulating me, too." She kisses him until Heather clears her throat. They break apart and we talk more about the logistics of Fern's departure. And then the meal is over, I've hugged my friend goodbye for now, and I find myself with absolutely nothing to do.

I have no idea how to relax, let alone have fun. I was going to work tomorrow, but my manager gave away my shift after I fainted and then called off. I'm about to climb the

Cathedral of Learning to stare out the windows at the city I'm leaving behind when my phone rings in my hand. Odin.

"Hello?" I know I told him I'd go out with him, but I wasn't expecting him to just call when I was on the verge of a meltdown.

"Congrats, grad. You are officially smarter than me."

I lean against the stone wall of the building, feeling the sunshine on my face. "I've always been smarter than you. Now I just have paperwork."

Odin's laugh is deep and slow. "What are you doing now? Wyatt just left with the rest of his shit, so I know you're not hanging with Fern."

I bite the inside of my cheek. I decide I don't have any reason to be coy or avoid the blatant truth. "I have no idea," I admit. "I have literally no plans."

He whoops. "I was hoping you'd say that," he says, voice urgent with excitement. "I have a really terrific idea if you're willing to drive my car for a bit."

I frown and push off the wall, walking toward a spot of shade. "What are you talking about?"

"Go pack an overnight bag and come to my place. I've got a top-notch celebration idea for us." I hesitate, confused by what he's asking. He continues, saying, "In fact, you don't even need to pack a bag if you don't want to. We'll just be naked. Come to my apartment."

"Odin Stag, you are insane. I am not going to be naked for an overnight trip."

"You better be naked for some of it, Janssen. Hurry your ass up and get here when you can." He hangs up before I can protest.

# CHAPTER 30
## ODIN

MY COUSIN WYATT took his girl to the family ski house for a romantic escape, and his fatal flaw was not checking the schedule to make sure nobody else would be there. I am committed to avoiding getting caught with my ass in the air by any member of the Stag family, so I cross out the next three days on the shared calendar.

I order a bunch of meal kits delivered to the house from a service local to the area, and I beg my brother to grab me a few bottles of wine from the store when he's out restocking on chips. By the time Thora hesitantly knocks on my door, I've packed the whole safe and satisfied basket along with a few outfits.

"Are you ready to be wined and dined?" I close the door behind me before she can engage Stellan or Gunnar in conversation.

Thora looks confused, so I hand her my knee roller and swing down the stairs. "The Stag family has a vacation house," I tell her. "It's like an hour from here. Super private. There's a hot tub."

She points to my cast. "Can you use a hot tub?"

I frown. "Good point. We'll just focus on other activities while we're there."

Thora squeezes around my backpack to open the front door of the apartment building, setting my scooter on the ground right outside the step. "What makes you think I want to be naked with you again?"

I wink at her. "I have so many more ideas for things we can do together, Thora Janssen. You are a college graduate. Don't you want to celebrate with the safe and satisfied basket?"

Her cheeks are pink, and I pull my car keys from my sweats pocket. I click to unlock my car and hoist myself inside as she tosses her bag in the back and climbs into the driver's seat. It takes her a long time to get it all the way up close enough that she can reach the pedals and see over the steering wheel. "Would it kill you to drive a car sized for regular people?"

I laugh. "You think you're regular-sized? You're fun-sized."

That has Thora roaring, and I'm glad I put her at ease. "Okay, you win. Tell me where to go." I direct her out of town and east on the turnpike for a few exits. We put the windows down and breathe in the mountain air when we get off the highway and wind our way along the curvy roads to the ski resort where our house is located at the top of the mountain.

"It's really quiet here in the summer," I promise. "There are people here for hiking and stuff, but there is absolutely nobody up on the slopes where the house is."

By the time Thora pulls into the driveway, she looks completely shell-shocked. I gotta admit, the house is pretty impressive. It's got a sloped roof and multi-story windows overlooking the woods. I hop out of the car and smile at the trio of meal boxes on the porch, which I shove inside the door with the front of my scooter. "Come on," I call to her. "Come see."

I grab her hand when she steps in the door, eyes wide at the sight of the great room. There's a remote-controlled fireplace along one wall and a massive sectional sofa. My favorite part is the huge wooden table that seats 20. She drops her bag on the floor and I tug her against my side, kissing her neck. "Welcome," I whisper. "Want a tour?"

She shakes her head, still staring.

I scratch at my chin, considering the open staircase leading up to most of the bedrooms. "Well, that's maybe okay because I don't think I can make it up to the second floor."

She chuckles. "I think we will be okay on this floor."

"There's a basement, too," I tell her. "That's where the foosball table is. And the theater room. And the hot tub, which we've already established I can't use…" My voice drifts off, and I stare out onto the deck, where the heated swimming pool is also off-limits while I'm still in the cast. Shit.

I let my hand trace along her arm as she looks around. "Are you okay? We can always play a game. Or watch a movie. I brought wine."

I stoop to pick up the bottle I shoved in the water bottle pocket of my backpack. I grin at Thora as I hold the alcohol, and she smiles, relaxing a bit. "Wine would be nice, I guess."

"You got it. Go sit." Thora folds herself onto the couch, looking smaller than ever, as I roll to the bar and grab us a few glasses. The wine is a screw top, which makes things really easy as I settle in next to her and pour us each a few inches. "To you," I tell her. "Congratulations."

She bites her lip. "I can't drink a toast to myself. That's weird."

I drape an arm around her, and she is receptive to that, so I scoot her closer to me. "What about…to relaxing?"

She clinks her glass to mine and nods. "To relaxing."

I reach for the remote and flick a button so the fireplace roars to life. She smiles and wiggles her toes as she sits cross-legged, leaning against me a little more. We sip in silence until she's put back about half her glass. "I still can't get over being done and having the grant. And not having to work. And—"

"Hey," I lean forward and set my wine on the table, turning to face Thora and putting a hand on each of her thighs. "You've had some big changes. Let me help you forget all that for a bit. Make you feel good." I let my fingers trace along her legs. She smells so nice, floral and leathery from my car, I guess. Or the couch cushions.

"What do you see in me? I'm mean to you." She leans back against the arm of the couch as I keep rubbing her legs. She sips the wine lazily and watches me touch her.

I grin. "You know I like it when you're mean to me." I stroke a finger behind each of her knees and she sucks in a breath. "And you like when I'm mean to you right back." I take the wine glass from her, set it on the table next to mine, and haul her onto my lap so she's pressed against my chest, face an inch from mine. "But how about if I'm nice to you for like a half hour?"

I swallow her laugh with a kiss and soon it's on like a remote-controlled fireplace. Thora wraps her arms around my neck as she presses her mouth into mine and I dig my fingers into her hips as I rock her on my length. "I'm so hard for you," I murmur into her mouth. And then I look at her face, eyes wild, so I bite her neck, and she gasps. "You like that? Do you get wet when I'm rough with you?"

I remember how I fantasized about fucking her against the wall, about bending her over and slamming into her from behind. I still can't do those things, but damn if I'm going to disappoint her while I have her on my lap. I pinch her nipples through her shirt because, of course she's not wearing a bra. Her hands scramble to pull off my t-shirt, and I reach an arm behind my head, pulling it off by the collar as she stares at me. I feel her nails drag along my abs, her tongue tracing the diamond in my earlobe. "I like all of it," she whispers, biting my ear as I pinch her nipples again.

She leans back to undo her jeans and yank them off while I work on my shorts. "Shit," I say. "The sex stuff is in my bag." I move to stand, thinking that I'll maybe hop over and get it, but she places a hand on my shoulder.

"I got it, Stag." And she saunters her tiny, naked ass over to my bag, strutting back over like some sort of sex goddess. She tosses it next to me on the couch. "Surprise me with your sack of goodies."

"Oh, honey, just you wait." I pull open the zipper. "Lie back." She arches a brow and does as I say. When one hand drops absentmindedly to her breast, I pop open a bottle of lube and squeeze a few drops between her fingers.

"What?" She gasps and then moans. "Oh, it's warm."

"Damn right," I tell her, smearing some more of it on my hands and massaging it into her nipples. And then I lap at one and then the other as she groans in disbelief. "And it's fucking cake flavored. Because this is a party."

# CHAPTER 31

# THORA

I'M LYING BACK on Odin Stag's magical guest couch while he licks my entire body, which he first spread with the warming lube.

I have never experienced this particular blend of sensations, and I don't know that I can go back to just regular feelings. This is twenty times better than the time I accidentally did coke at a party in high school and felt like a million bucks making out with a football player.

I guess I'm making out with a bigger, better football player now. And then I shut that thought down because, of course, Odin's badly injured. His cast bumps against my leg as a reminder as he works his way up from my pussy to my chest like he can't make up his mind where he'd rather linger.

And then he kisses me, and I can taste myself and the flavored lube, and I groan into his mouth. I'm falling to pieces right here underneath him, but his body is holding me together. "I want you so much," I pant, and he nods, grinning. He's so beautiful up close, even more so when he looks at me like I'm simultaneously made of glass and the most amazing thing he's ever seen.

"Look at you," he says, running a finger down my ribs,

across my pelvis, inserting it inside my body, which welcomes the thick digit. "You're dying for it."

"Yes," I stutter. "I already said that. Come on, Stag." He laughs and reaches into the bag, pulling out a strip of condoms. "What all do you have in there?"

"Patience, Thora. You want my Spear of Heaven or not?" He starts to roll on the condom as he laughs at his own joke. I admire him, naked and gorgeous, kneeling between my legs while he douses his sheathed cock in lube.

And then he slides inside me, warm and slippery, and I gasp because I feel so full and so damn hot. "Odin." My breath comes in pants as my hands grip his shoulders. He moans, nibbling at my shoulders with his perfect teeth, while he starts to thrust. I think the couch surface makes it easier for him to find traction with his cast, which he seems to have wedged against the back cushions.

He starts to rub at my clit, and I stop caring about his injury. I can't care about anything at all when he makes me feel this way, and it occurs to me that I just might be able to come without a vibrator if he can just keep doing that thing with his thumb while he thrusts. "Odin, don't stop. Please, I'm so close."

"Yeah?" He pulls his head back to look at me but continues to apply pressure with his thumb.

"Yes!" I squeeze with all my might, wrapping my legs around his waist. And I feel it starting. "Odin, I'm going to come. Just like that. Oh, Odin, it's happening." I think I start to cry as my body begins to pulse and shudder and gulp him in. I stare into his eyes, and it's just as intense as before, except it's warm and different, my eyes roll back in my head as the sparks of pleasure careen up and down my spine.

I think I'm screaming his name. I think I'm kicking his butt cheeks with my heels, like he's a horse I'm riding into battle.

"Fuck, Odin, shit." I'm panting. He's grinning and his thumb is still pressed against my clit as the waves subside.

"You came," he whispers, his hips still, cock twitching inside me.

"I did." I groan and poke his shoulder like I need to check if he's real. "You made me."

"I helped you." He plants a kiss on my nose. "You ready for more?"

I snap my eyes back to his and bite my lip. He's still hard, after all. He hasn't come. Could I do that a second time? "I want to try."

"That's my girl." He kisses me again and starts moving. Our eyes are locked together as he bites his lip in concentration. "Mmm, it's so wet."

I stare at the bottle of lube on the coffee table, noting its location in case we need more of it. And then I thrust my hips up to meet his, grinding myself against his pelvis while he lets out small sounds of pleasure...I don't even know he's aware of producing.

"Does this feel good? What do you like?" I want to make him explode just like he did to me. I want to pull him over that cliff with me.

He pauses his movement, props himself on one elbow, and traces my nipple with a finger. "Remember when you played with my ass?"

I laugh. "How could I forget? The sound you made was epic."

He flicks his gaze to the lube. "Would you want to do that again?"

I frown momentarily. "I'm not ready to lick back there if that's what you're thinking."

"No," he shakes his head. "I just meant...it felt really good. Your finger. And the lube is so nice..."

I reach for the bottle with one hand, tilting my chin to see above his shoulder as I squirt some into my hand.

He smiles as I set the bottle on the carpet and reach for his butt while he moves inside me. "Your ass is so firm." I pinch it with my dry hand.

"For now, I guess. Oh, shit, Thora." I slide a finger in between his cheeks and trace a hand down as low as I can reach. I curl up so my arm has more purchase, and I can just manage to tap the tight pucker that gives way as he buries himself deep into my body.

Our eyes connect as I gently slide my slippery finger inside his body, and his mouth drops open. Odin's entire frame begins to shudder, and he roars. I feel his cock swell and throb, and he just keeps on yelling, coming almost violently inside me until he drops his hand between my legs again, pressing my clit until another orgasm seizes me, too. My hand slips out from its exploration as I come in gasping waves. When it's over, I sink into the couch, and he collapses on top of me.

Heaving and panting, we hold each other until moving almost seems possible again.

# CHAPTER 32
## ODIN

"THAT WAS INTENSE." After we fucked, I dragged Thora down the hall to the bathroom and ordered her to get into the giant whirlpool tub, where I can dangle one leg out the side and pull her between my legs so she's lying back against my chest while the water swirls around us.

"Mmm. I liked it." Her eyes are closed, and she lets me play with her tits all I want, which is constantly. I could lie here like this for hours, a gorgeous woman in my lap, rock-hard nipples in my palms. "Where did you get cake-flavored lube?"

I shrug, adjusting my weight so I can shut off the water with my good foot. "It was in the basket. I don't ask questions. Maybe Stellan added that one."

She shifts so she can see me, resting her cheek on my chest, which also feels awesome. "Did you take the whole basket?"

"I dumped and ran, baby." She laughs. I kiss the top of her head like I'm allowed to do that. Like she's mine. Except I know she's not. We're here right now because she took a big step on a journey that's leading her far away from me. But I don't want to think about that right now.

She settles back in between my legs. I should be alarmed that I'm not getting wood again, but I came harder than I ever did in my life, so I'll chalk it up as a win if I can get there again after dinner. "So, I've seen the couch and the bathroom. You're telling me the other floors of this place are even nicer?"

"The nicest. You can go look around later. I'm going to cook dinner, and that'll take a while."

Thora sits up, and I hate it, so I pull her back, wanting her soft skin against me. "Odin," she says, "I'm not going to wander around your family's house without you."

I run my fingers through her hair, getting it wet so I can wash it like she did for me back at my place. "It's not like you're trespassing. But if you don't want to see the bunk room, that's your loss."

"I'm not sleeping in a bunk bed." She tips her head back, giving me more access to get her hair wet, and I reach for the shampoo, pouring some in my hand and starting to work it into her dark hair. It's straight and smooth between my fingers, and now she smells like soap instead of sex and lube.

"You better not sleep in the bunk bed. I was thinking we probably wouldn't sleep at all." She hums, and I wash her hair, then nudge her to scoot down further in the water so I can use my hands to cup water over it and rinse everything. Eventually, she turns, and we wash each other's bodies with the soap, her nipples impossibly hard, dragging along my chest when she leans forward to wash my back. Is she loving this as much as I am?

"Tell me about your travel plans," I tell her, to get my mind off the word "love" and the creeping feeling of attachment that is overtaking my brain.

Thora smiles. Her face is clean and bright and pink from the hot water. Or the sex. Or both. "I have everything set up," she tells me. "Passport. Visa. Ticket. I fly out on August 1, and Fern is meeting me at the airport. Which is good because my plane gets in super late at night, and I don't want to take the bus alone at one in the morning."

I frown at this. "You better not take a bus alone at one in the morning."

She swats at me. "I just said I wasn't. Wyatt has a car." Suddenly, I hate that my cousin will see my girl when she embarks on her life goal. My girl…that's not fair. I haven't earned the right to call her mine. We're just messing around while she waits for her next step, and I figure out what the hell my life looks like now.

I realize she has continued talking, and I lace my fingers together behind my head while she sits facing me in the giant tub. My leg is half asleep from dangling out of the tub, but I have my whole life to improve my circulation. This is my only chance to see Thora Janssen excited about international scholar orientation at Oxford.

"And then I'm pretty much on my own in the library," she says, clasping her hands together under her chin. She rests her elbows on my knees, and I press my legs together, pinning her in place. She giggles. I love it. "Nine entire months just learning about international family law and social services policy. I'm going to draw correlations and bring it all with me to law school. It would be great to do a Master's in Public Policy, too…what?"

She tucks her hair behind her ears. I shake my head. "Nothing. I just like hearing you talk about this stuff."

"You and Fern and nobody else." She sighs. "All right. I'm turning into a prune. You said you'd feed me."

Thora flicks the drain on the tub and the water starts gurgling out. "I guess you're in a hurry for my hot beef."

"Oooh, I do enjoy steamy meat." She cracks up as she steps out of the tub and, to my frustration, covers her body in a fluffy towel. "Do you need help getting out?"

I wish I could tell her I didn't. I wish I could do a lot of things, but I accept her hand and swing myself out of the tub, leaning against the side of it while I dry off.

Thora follows me to the kitchen, chatting about her packing plans while she pulls clothes from her bag and, unfortunately, covers up. I tug on a pair of shorts and start prepping one of the meal kits while we drink wine. It feels so natural, teasing her, talking about random shit like whether she needs compression socks for an international flight. "You're not middle-aged with circulation issues, Thora. I think you'll be fine."

She sips her drink. "I've never flown before at all...how should I know?"

"You never flew anywhere?" I offer her a spoon to taste the pan sauce while the meat simmers on the stove.

She closes her eyes and nods. "That's good. And no. I've never really left Pittsburgh much."

I think about my own childhood, traveling all over the world for my extended family's sports adventures. But none of that has prepared me for a future once my life got derailed. Thora has built herself a bulletproof plan, all within the confines of the Steel City.

I plate the food and realize I can't easily carry it all to the table, so I slide the plates onto the counter, and Thora hops up into one of the stools. We eat side by side, talking about nothing and everything until she slides her plate away, drops a hand to my crotch, and tells me to show her our bedroom.

# CHAPTER 33
# THORA

I ABSOLUTELY CANNOT GET USED to this. What is this life where I'm swept off to a luxury cabin with a man who not only makes me come but cooks me dinner and plies me with delicious wine? I wake up cocooned in crisp, soft linens that smell so fresh and clean. And I've got a warm, hairy arm around my waist again, with Odin breathing softly into my hair as he holds me tight.

Maybe I can appreciate it for what it is: a perfect getaway. A gift for my graduation. Although, based on the sounds he was making last night again in bed, this is as much a reward for Odin as it is for me. We used that entire bottle of lube.

My body alerts me to the need to use the bathroom, and I struggle to free myself from his iron grasp. I eye the giant tub in the mirror as I fix my hair and brush my teeth. Did we really spend an hour in there just talking about my future? I realize I didn't ask him anything about his rehab or what comes next for him.

And then I gaze at his sleeping form and realize that was probably by design. Maybe this is an escape for him from thinking about all of that. I know his family is giving him a lot of pressure to make decisions and fill out paperwork. I heard

Fern and Wyatt talking about that, and Odin has hinted at a few things.

I decide he deserves some more time to just mindlessly enjoy some pleasure, so I crawl my way back into the bed and reach in between his legs.

I find him hot and hard, and I smile, giving him a few pumps before I wrap my mouth around the tip of his cock. His eyes fly open, and he looks down at me, stunned, face-melting into utter joy as I plant kisses all along his shaft.

"Morning," I whisper, wrapping one hand around the base of his cock while I do my best to fit him into my mouth.

"Are you serious right now? Wow." Odin bites his lip, staring as I manage to get a few inches of his length inside my throat before I hollow out my cheeks and give a good, hard suck. "Oh, Thora. Gorgeous. Wow."

His hand drops to my hair, reverent, as he stares at me. I release him with a wet pop as I catch my breath and then hold his gaze while I suck with all my might, bobbing my head up and down, pumping him with one hand and cradling his balls with the other.

His body goes limp as Odin leans into the sensations, but soon enough, I feel him stiffen everywhere. "Thora, honey, I'm gonna—"

He tries to lift my head from his dick, but I send him a look. I know what I'm doing. I want to drink down the reward for this work. I want to make Odin Stag crumble to pieces because of me, and I want to be here to lick it all better at the end.

I wriggle my shoulders a bit so my nipples graze along his thighs, and that extra stimulation sends him right over the edge. Odin roars, one strong hand digging into the sheets while the other remains gentle in my hair. He spurts into my mouth, salty and hot, and I swallow down his release gladly. I want to get used to this. I cannot get used to this.

But there's today. And there's right now. And as I release

Odin's softening cock, I stare into his blue eyes and see this massive man has fallen apart right here in bed beside me. It's a lot. But I chose this, and damn it, I'm going to soak it in.

"Morning," I tell him again.

He can't form words. He smiles lazily and pats the pillow beside him. I crawl back up and figure I'm going to rest my head next to him, maybe fall asleep some more, but he pulls me on top of him and kisses me, moaning into my mouth, pressing his lips into mine like he wants to fuse us together. "You're incredible," he says, tracing my chin with his finger, cupping the side of my face like I'm a treasured thing.

I can't speak, so I rest my cheek on his chest until his breathing slows, and he falls back asleep.

———

I don't remember falling back asleep, but I wake up to the smell of food cooking. I pad down the hall in Odin's t-shirt. He notices from behind the stove where he's folding an omelet onto a plate. "You better be naked beneath that," he says, tugging off his robe. He is, like before, just wearing athletic shorts. I like the opportunity to stare at this perfect specimen of the human body.

Well. Perfect, plus one small, injured part.

I sigh and hop up onto a stool. I sort of like eating at the counter with him this way. It's cozy despite the enormity of the house. "So, what's the deal with this place again? Who owns it?"

He hops up next to me and rests his cast on another stool. "My dad and his three brothers bought it together for Uncle Tim's 40th birthday. Now we all share it."

I look around the walls, covered in black and white photographs of a truly astounding number of boy children. "And you said there's a calendar for it?"

He nods. "And I double-checked." He squeezes my thigh

and then lifts the hem of the shirt, peeking. I swat his hand away, and he laughs. "The whole family was all supposed to be at graduation this weekend." He takes a sip of juice. "Wes, Wyatt, and me. We were all going to graduate, and now... none of us did. Life is strange that way, I guess."

I hesitate, but since he brought it up, I decide to ask anyway. "What will you do about school?"

He nods, chewing and swallowing his eggs. He seems a little sad that his plate is empty, and I slide mine toward him. There's no way I can eat all this food anyway. He looks wide-eyed at my offering. "You sure?" When I nod, he continues talking. "Well, I finally did talk to my advisors. I got extensions for my classes. All except argument. Thank you very much for the motivation to get an A in that one."

I hold up my juice cup in a toast, and he clinks it against mine. "So anyway, in addition to a whole bunch more rehab, my big summer plans include geography homework and essays about sociology."

I finish my juice and dab at my mouth, hesitating again. "And then?"

"Then I have no fucking idea." He throws down his fork. "I can't play. I'm not even sure I'll be walking by fall. I'm just buying time until I figure out what the future looks like for a has-been athlete with no other marketable skills."

"Hey, don't say that." He scoffs. "I mean, you are an okay cook."

That draws a laugh out of him. I can't help but add, "it's nice that you can take some time, though. You know that you have support."

He nods. "Wyatt said something the other day that sort of stuck with me...but I don't know if it's possible."

My brows lift. "What? Tell me!" It's exciting to think he might have even a kernel of an idea for his next steps.

Odin blows a raspberry. "It's dumb. Maybe. But he said his team in London has a whole staff of mental health pros."

I clap my hands. "Sports psychology is a real thing for sure. You could go to grad school for that."

He shoulders me. "She says to the college dropout."

I shoulder him right back. "You just said you're fixing that, though. And don't get a big head or anything, but you're pretty decent at research and papers. That's most of grad school."

He grins at me. "Was that a compliment, Janssen?"

I throw my napkin at him, and he catches it mid-air. "This is my thanks? And I went to bat for you…" He stops mid-sentence and shakes his head.

"What do you mean?" I frown as Odin slides our plates toward the sink and pivots over there on his scooter, rinsing the dishes and setting them in the dishwasher. "Odin, what do you mean you went to bat? About what?"

"I didn't mean that. There was no bat." He starts hand washing the pan he used to cook the eggs in, and then he seems to change his mind. "Come outside on the deck with me," he says, starting to roll toward the sliding door. "Let's enjoy the view."

I can tell he's trying to change the subject, but in the spirit of enjoying myself, I follow him. The air is crisp here. I can hear birds and insects. I close my eyes and soak in the differences from the city. I wonder if this is what the scenery will be like at Oxford. If London is a similar city to Pittsburgh, what will life be like over there?

He wraps an arm around my shoulder and squeezes. "Pretty nice, right? I wish we could swim."

I frown at the pool. "Wouldn't it be freezing?"

He shakes his head. "Heated."

I roll my eyes. "I should have figured. Fancy-ass family." I sigh and stare over the deck railing at the trees beyond the currently grassy ski slopes. But then I think more about Odin's wealthy family and what he said at the sink. My stomach is uneasy. Something is off. I remember him showing up at the diploma ceremony, the way my advisor insisted I be there for a surprise award. A shiver rolls down my neck as I start to put it all together. "Hey, what did you mean? About going to bat."

He shakes his head and grips the deck rail. He is hiding something. "Did you have something to do with that scholarship? Is that why you and your mom were there at the ceremony?"

Odin grips the edge of the counter. "You're an amazing student, Thora. You deserve that money and more. You're doing good things in the world. I felt terrible that you paid your mom's rent so she'd come to graduation."

I fly back from the rail, horrified. "You felt bad?"

He throws a hand in the air. "Of course, I felt bad for you!"

I press my knuckles to my temples. All this has been way too good to be true. And now I see it for what it all was. "Am I your pity project? Is that what I am to you?"

"Thora. No. Wait. You're getting this wrong."

I cross my arms and stare up at him. "Then tell me what's right. Tell me you had nothing to do with that money."

He scratches the back of his neck. "Look," he starts, and I shriek and tug at my hair. I'm going to have to pay it back. I feel disgusting and cheap. I never wanted to be the object of anyone's pity, let alone a man I'm sleeping with. "Thora, I don't even know what the fuck I was going to do with that money otherwise. I can't live up to the expectations that were set when I got it from the fucking video game people."

I growl at him. I want to shove him in the chest but I'm adult enough not to knock him over while he's injured. "Odin, you can't just *sneak* and trick me. How am I supposed to react when I learn your entire family was talking about me? About how unfortunate I am?"

I groan and rush into the house, down the hall to the bedroom. I have to pack my stuff. I have to get out of here.

Somehow. If I have to walk back to Pittsburgh, so be it. I hear him rolling down behind me. "I only gave some of the money. The rest was legitimately from lawyers all over the damn city who were impressed by you, Thora. It all went through the women's law clinic, I swear. It's a real award."

"Don't patronize me," I snap. "I've spent my entire life being patronized by people who think they know what's best for me. I thought you were different."

"Thora, please," Odin pleads. "I was just trying to help. My family has so much, and you work so hard—"

"Stop. Just stop." I hold up a hand. "I don't need you to remind me how hard my life is compared to yours. I don't need your family's pity money."

"It's not pity! God, you're so stubborn about accepting help—"

"And you're so used to throwing money at problems that you don't understand why this hurts me!" I ball my hands into fists and shake my head. "You know what the worst part is? I actually started to believe I maybe deserved good things. That I earned them on my merit. But this whole time, you were just another person who saw me as someone to fix." I tug at my hair. "I trusted you, Odin. What a mistake."

"Please sit so we can talk about this," he begs, hopping over to the bed and sitting next to my bag, where I'm stuffing in clothes and toiletries. "You're the only thing I have going for me right now, Thora."

I shake my head and yank off his shirt, stuffing my own over my head instead. "That's not fair, Odin. Everyone in my life depends on me utterly and fully. I thought you were someone I could maybe lean on."

"You can! That's why I wanted—"

I snarl. "Don't tell me that's why you gave me money. Just forget it. You'll never, ever understand where I'm coming from. I don't have a family who will pay my rent while I figure out my shit. I don't have anyone, Odin. I need to get out of here."

His face falls, and he breathes quietly for a few beats. "Take the car," he says. "My family can come get me."

I roll my eyes. "Of course they can." I groan and huff past him. "I'll leave your keys with your brother or whoever I can find."

I pause at the door, tears burning my eyes. "You know what kills me? I actually let myself believe you saw me as an equal. But I was just your charity case all along."

"Thora, that's not—"

"Save it for the next hard-luck case you want to rescue."

I slam the door to the palace in the mountains and cry the entire drive back to the city. When I get to Odin's apartment, I ring the bell, slap the keys into Gunnar's palm, and stalk off down the road as he shouts my name and asks what happened. Let him call Odin and ask.

# CHAPTER 34
# ODIN

A FEW HOURS LATER, all three of my brothers showed up to retrieve me. I didn't even call them, but since they arrived in my car, I guess Thora had already seen them and gone.

"Hey, man," Gunny says, sinking into the couch beside me. I don't even have the television on. I'm just staring into the fireplace, trying to figure out where I went so wrong. Thora thinks I pity her, but the opposite is true. I revere her. I find her to be extraordinary.

That feels like a bougie word, but it's the best I can think of. And I've spent hours just sitting here thinking about it.

I grunt at my brothers as the twins squeeze in on my other side.

Gunnar stretches and puts an arm around my shoulder. "Sooooo Thora stopped by...looked pretty pissed."

I nod and cross my arms. Alder and Tucker trade farts, probably trying to get a reaction from me, but I'm used to their antics.

Gunnar sighs. "We wanted to talk to you, actually. And since you weren't with Thora and you don't really leave the house, we tracked your phone."

Tucker nods. "Did you know I always know where you are, bro?"

I shrug, still not looking over at him and Alder. I'm sure Dad has our whole family tracked just in case, but I don't say so.

Gunny sighs. "We've been thinking about you and your bum leg, man. And our careers."

I frown and spare a glance at my brother. "What do you mean?"

He retracts his arm and pats my thigh. "You know hockey is different from football. I signed with the Fury two years ago."

"I know that." I still think it's weird that hockey drafts guys while they're still in college and waits around for them to finish before they start with the pros. And then it occurs to me that I think that's weird because guys can get injured. Seriously injured. Like me. "What are you saying?"

Gunny nods. "I'm leaving school." He points to the twins. "We all are. The twins got drafted in January. We don't want..." He drifts off without saying *we don't want to wind up like you*.

I pinch my lips together.

Alder winces. "We just...want at least a million bucks if we're going to get hurt anyway."

Tucker grunts. "Maybe you're only getting a million."

They start to argue about who is getting the better offer, and I hop up to my foot and extract myself from the couch.

"Odin, wait." Gunnar looks serious. "We wanted you to know that, like, this isn't all in vain. Or whatever."

I close my eyes and shake my head. "Gee. Thanks. Can you take me home now?"

Alder grunts, and I stare at him. "Mom said to drop you at the boathouse."

They start to walk toward the door of the ski house.

Tucker asks, "Do you need to do anything? Burn the sheets? Scour the countertops?"

"I stripped the bed, jagoff." I pull the door shut behind me, and Alder types in the code to lock up.

"What the hell am I going to do at the boathouse?" I climb into the back seat of my own car. Tucker drives, and Alder sits up front with him. I don't want to interrupt their twin vibe. They're lucky they got drafted to the same team, so they can stay joined at the brain.

They're just all-around lucky… unlike me.

Gunny sings along to the radio for a few bars and then says, "I'm assuming you'll explain to Mom how you fucked up with Thora. Or maybe she'll make you work out with her. I don't know, man. I'm just following orders."

It's a weird, fast drive back into the city. I fall asleep for half of it and wake up with my face pressed against the window as my brother pulls off the highway onto the bridge toward Washington's Landing, where Mom keeps her fancy boats.

She used to take all of us out with her. Now, she mostly rows alone. But she's waiting in the parking lot as my brother rolls to a stop. I leave my bag in the car and grab my scooter from the back as the guys wave to Mom, who blows them kisses and then turns to me with a weird smile. "Come see what I have for you."

She heads down the ramp from the parking lot to the boat house, and I follow her, trying not to let the scooter roll away from me on the slope. Mom gestures at a boat propped on slings in the middle of the room. "Ta-da!"

I furrow my brow. "It's a boat."

She grins. "It's an adaptive rowing boat! I talked to your trainer and—"

"Mom, they're not supposed to just talk to you. What the hell? Don't I have privacy or something?"

She rolls her eyes. "I didn't discuss your particular situation. I asked what sort of rowing someone might try after an Achilles repair. This boat has a regular seat for me, and I set one up for you with just one foot pad. We'll each use two oars..."

I tune out as she babbles about how we will both hop in the river and splash our way around the island ten or twenty times. I don't bother to point out that I can't help her carry the boat to the dock, but she surprises me by unlocking little wheels on the boat slings. She's whistling her way down the ramp before I can respond, and she hoists the boat into the water on her own, reminding me that my mom is still jacked.

I scratch my chin and stare as she sets the oars up near the boat. "How will I get in? This is all awkward..."

Mom braces herself on the dock and tells me to squat low and take her hand. I do and step into the boat with my good leg, which is not the leg closest to the water. "You couldn't set up the boat in the other direction?" I grumble and clench my core as the boat rocks.

Mom steadies it with one foot. "Just sit down, kid."

I lower my butt into the seat, acknowledging that this is already a fantastic workout just climbing aboard. Mom is in her element in the seat behind me. "All right, O. Grab your oars. You remember. Yes, now strap your left foot to the boards. I set the footpad as big as it goes. I hope it works okay for your monster feet."

I grunt at her and get myself situated. I haven't rowed with her for a long time, but we sometimes do the rowing machine for workouts with football, and I'm sure my technique is still good. Mom pushes us off the dock, and when I glance over my shoulder, she's pretty much just holding the boat steady while I do all the work. She grins at me. "Doesn't the burn feel good, baby? Do you miss it?"

I glower at her because she's right. This feels amazing. My

work at physical therapy has been very focused on small movements for my ankle. Then, I'm sometimes allowed to do seated upper body workouts, and if I'm very, very polite, Prachi lets me do one-legged squats.

But this is grabbing every part of my body except my right leg. I feel the movements in my hips. I feel my whole back working the oars in the river, and when I lean back, I feel the sun on my face as I dig in, which gets us going a little faster. "All right," I admit. "This is nice."

Mom chuckles and starts bossing me around like she's the coxswain. She must have already worked out today because otherwise, I don't think she'd be able to stand just sitting there holding her oars out of the way. We make a full lap around the island before she joins in, confident I'm not going to tip the boat with my uneven pressure.

We do two more laps before she calls it, and we approach the dock. There, we do the whole dance in reverse to get me out of the boat and the boat back up on the slings.

I lean heavily on my knee roller as I follow her. "That was pretty good, Mom. I'm sorry I was a jerk about it."

She smiles. "Just wait until you can walk on that cast. One of the guys from the masters team is an orthopedic surgeon. He thinks you could be rowing fully, regularly, by October."

I chew on the inside of my cheek. I haven't let myself think about October or anything beyond finishing my spring semester classes. Even that's new for me ever since my body broke.

"Mom, October is...I don't even know where I'll be living in August."

She beckons me to follow her to her car and helps me get my scooter in the back seat. Once we're both buckled inside, she turns on the air and says, "I was thinking about that, too. I know how much you love team sports. Did you know they have a crew team at Oxford?"

My eyes fly wide. "Mom, what did you do?" Thora's already furious with me for helping her fly to England. She will murder me if I show up there on the crew team. "I can't just enroll at Oxford. I didn't even finish college."

Mom waves a hand and puts the car in gear, heading back toward the bridge to the highway. "You'll finish your classes in a few weeks. Did you know the dean of admissions at Oxford was an Olympic rower, too?" I snort at my mother, who apparently has a PhD in meddling. Mom nods. "She's a little younger than me, but we're on the same online forums."

"Mom. You are insane. I can't just move to England and row boats now that I'm done playing football."

She scoffs like I'm the one being ridiculous. "Why not? You love team sports. You're an accomplished athlete. And you need a little time to figure out your next steps in the world. What's the harm in a little master's degree?"

"Okay," I pat her hand. "Let's pretend this idea isn't utterly ridiculous. Why Oxford? Why aren't you sending me to your old stomping grounds in Boston or something?"

She rolls her eyes, absolutely fed up with my apparent stupidity. "Two reasons, kid. First, you can compete for your university as a graduate student in the UK. Second, you can go win back your girl!"

Like it's so easy. Like she'd ever consider being mine. But Mom's idea does rekindle the curiosity Wyatt set off about a career in sports psychology. Who better to step into that role than someone who has walked that walk?

Mom drops me off at my apartment, where Wyatt's room is totally empty, Gunnar is half packed, and I realize that I'm powerless against the river of change flowing through my life.

Maybe my mom's idea isn't so ridiculous. It certainly beats living in my parents' basement while I figure out what comes next for me. Oxford is a big place. If Thora tells me to go pound sand, our paths don't need to cross. And I can get to some of Wyatt's games while I'm over there figuring out how to walk again.

I text Thora that I'm sorry, I'm here if she's willing to talk, and I lock myself in my room to scrape together a passing set of grades for the semester that just ended.

# CHAPTER 35
# THORA

ODIN TEXTS once a week to apologize and ask to talk. And I have zero time to deal with that nonsense. I'm too busy working double shifts all summer trying to pay him back for his pity portion of that scholarship. I can begrudgingly accept that most of the money came from actual charitable sources. Still, Fern confirmed that Odin donated his endorsement money from some video game to his uncle's foundation and told them to launder the money until it became a scholarship. For me.

It's embarrassing to think about the way I thought we were connecting, but he was actually just feeling sorry for the poor girl with formerly-incarcerated parents. God, what must he have been thinking about when I thought our eyes were locking, connecting despite our differences.

He and his savior complex can fuck right off. Which, I guess he did already. I don't know why I keep hoping he'll turn up at the bar. It's not like I've given him any hope of connecting. His family is probably vacationing in Ibiza or something glamorous. No, cancel that. They're probably all up in their mountain palace.

"Thora!" My manager snaps her fingers, and I shake out

of my thought spiral. I've been on thin ice here at work despite years of dedicated work behind the bar. One little dizzy spell and one call-off...on arguably the busiest night of the year for a college bar...has put me in the doghouse for the whole summer.

I'm making bank right now, though, so I can't complain. I'm giving a lot of it to my parents and setting aside big chunks to pay Odin back as soon as I can figure out how to get him the money in a way he can't refuse or sneak back to me somehow. Fern says I'm being stubborn about this.

I'm counting down the days until I can see her again.

———

At the end of July, I work my last shift and untie my apron for the final time. I take the bus home, and since I'm leaving in the morning, I realize this might be my last time seeing this part of the city for a long time. I'll be different when I get back here. I press a palm to the window and stare at the streets below the Bloomfield Bridge. I look at the hospitals and university buildings that have defined my view my entire life. Everything that once felt so out of reach is finally within my grasp.

I pack the last of my things into my two new-to-me suitcases, and in the morning, I wake up earlier than I need to in search of my mother.

She's in the kitchen, wearing her work uniform, crying. "Oh," she says. "Hey, sweetheart."

"Mom." I wrap my arms around her slim, tired frame. I hear the familiar gurgle of the coffeemaker and try to imprint that aroma as my main memory of this house, of my childhood. "I wish you could come with me."

Mom snorts. "Yeah, right. Me travel abroad."

I pull back and stare at her. "You could visit me. I could help you get your passport. I'd help you."

She smiles and smooths my hair. "Thora, baby, I'm not cut out for that kind of stress. But it makes me proud knowing you'll be out there, showing them what Pittsburgh girls can be."

I lean against her shoulder, thinking how desperately I wish I could help her more, how her circumstances inspire my entire research focus, my fellowship application...everything. I consider that Odin maybe, could have felt similarly. But then I let that thought slip away so I can kiss my mother goodbye and splurge on a car service to the airport.

———

The flight is long and confusing for me. Am I supposed to tip the flight attendants who bring me free wine and food every few hours? Do people really pay extra for internet access when we have an entire library of free movies to choose from?

I keep my nose down, repeatedly clutch at my passport tucked into my bra, and finally make my way through customs and into the bustle of Heathrow's airport, which doesn't feel at all different from the crowded T station in downtown Pittsburgh after a hockey game.

My heart flutters in my chest as I search for Fern, and then I see her holding a giant sign with my name on it. She jumps up and down, hollering, and people stare. But who cares? We can be obnoxious Americans for a minute. "You're here," Fern squeals.

"You're here," I squeal back. And we dance in a circle around my bags, two scholarship girls from Pittsburgh here in London for graduate school. "This is surreal," I whisper.

She nods. "Come on." She grabs one of my bags. "Wyatt sent a car for us."

I chuckle. "Of course he did. It sucks that he's away. I

would have given him a handshake or something to thank him."

She laughs and guides me toward a black car with a driver in a suit, eager to grab my bags and open our doors. It's a bit weird getting in a car with the steering wheel on the right, but I'm too tired to focus on it for long.

"You don't have to thank Wyatt," Fern says. "This is just something he likes to do to take care of me."

I run my arms along the leather interior. "Yeah, but you have to admit it's...maybe weird is the wrong word. But it's very different from what we're used to."

She smiles and closes her eyes, resting her head against the cushy seatback. "I take care of him, too."

"Gross, Fern." I swat at her leg, and she laughs.

"Not like that. Seriously. Our relationship is very reciprocal. We have different love languages." I wish her comment didn't immediately make me think of Odin, causing my entire body to clench uncomfortably. I'm quiet for a bit, staring out the window as some of the city sights come into view. Fern says, "Hey, Geoffrey, can you make sure we pass The Eye? I want Thora to see it."

"You got it, guv," the driver says, winking at us in the rearview mirror. I keep my eyes focused out the window.

"Anyway," Fern says, "Wyatt is very generous with people he cares about. Which includes you because you're important to me."

I sigh. "Thank you. Thank him for me. You're important to me, too."

"Duh," she says. And then she drops a bomb: "And you're maybe important to other people in the Stag family, too..."

"Don't." I shake my head. "I can't." She's going to bring up Odin, and my heart can't handle all the conflicted feelings I have about him. He was supposed to be a spring fling, anyway.

"Why?" She pokes my shoulder. "He's kind of perfect for

you. He gives you shit, and he's competitive like you. And he's smitten, Thora. Anyone could see…"

I turn to face her, spying the giant Ferris wheel Fern mentioned all lit up out her side of the car. "Okay, well, he's also super pushy and lives in a different country and has no life plan beyond living in his parents' basement." She bites her lip. I frown at her. "What? What do you know?"

She winces. "He doesn't live in his parents' basement."

"Oh. Okay, so he's still in a shitty athlete apartment playing video games."

"You like video games."

"Ugh!" I flop back in my seat and close my eyes. "That's not the point."

Her hand drops to mine and squeezes. I flip my palm over and squeeze back, wrapping our fingers together, enjoying being physically in my best friend's presence again, even if she's choosing right now to pester me about my spring fling.

"He's doing a master's in sports psychology," she whispers.

I open my eyes and stare at her in the dark, illuminated by the city lights, remembering what he said about that fledgling idea for his future before he revealed that he saw me as a charity project. "Well," I spit out. "That's fucking awesome." And it's true, but unexpected. "I love that for him." This last bit comes out with less vehemence.

The car eases to a stop outside a gorgeous apartment building, brightly lit by streetlights, with little awnings over the windows and flower boxes and a doorman in a red uniform. "You should text him," Fern says, unbuckling and accepting Geoffrey's hand as she exits the car.

"I'll think about it," I tell her, and I follow her upstairs to check out her incredible flat.

# CHAPTER 36
## THORA

ALL THE MELATONIN in the world couldn't put me to sleep this week. My body is wrecked with the time change. I eventually gave up trying to sleep at Fern's house and just stared out her flat windows at the London streets at night. The city isn't so very different from Pittsburgh…neighborhoods built and bisected by a river…cobblestones and old architecture sprinkled with new bike lanes and modern parks. It makes me feel at home in a way.

In the morning, Fern—well, with Geoffrey—drives me to Oxford and holds my hand while I sign in for the graduate student housing. I'm living in a glorious old building full of wee flats. My place is one room with a bathroom, tiny kitchen, and nook for the bed tucked in the wall where I can stare up at the beautiful wooden ceiling or stare out the window of the sandstone building.

I don't have much to unpack, and the kitchen comes equipped with *very* basic supplies…so Fern gives me a watery-eyed hug and heads back to her own school. The flat has built-in drawers and bookshelves, although I didn't bring any books to put on them. I fantasize about acquiring some while I'm here...old law texts and reference guides to policies from all the different nations that prioritize social services.

I fall back on the bed, clapping my hands, and pass out in the middle of the afternoon, which isn't going to do my jet lag any favors.

I wake up groggy in the middle of the night, and by four in the morning, I'm wide awake and ready to face my day. Too bad it doesn't begin for five more hours. I decide to teach myself about English tea and boil some water in the kettle on my tiny stove. I'm feeling very posh, pouring it into a pot with loose leaves Fern gifted me, but stirring and sipping in silence just leads to thoughts of Odin.

Honestly, I don't know what to make of the new information I've learned and processed. He figured out what he wants to do. He leveraged his family's wealth to do something nice for me. He told me I'm the only thing he has going right in his life. It's all too much, too soon, when I need to clear space in my head for this fellowship.

I will call him. Or text him. Eventually, I still intend to give him back his portion of that grant money. I even set it aside in a sub-account in my shiny new international checking account.

———

After two showers and a long session ironing my first-day outfit, I shoulder my laptop bag, toe on my red flats, and walk to orientation, knowing I look like what I am: a professional young woman starting graduate school.

The sun is shining, which I wasn't expecting, but I tuck my new raincoat in my bag regardless. I sign in for international student programming and mill around munching an actual crumpet.

"And where are you from?" A guy with a French accent holds a hand out toward me, a hopeful smile on his face.

"Pittsburgh. In the States," I tell him, shaking his hand and smiling. Look at me mingling. This isn't terribly different from bartending. Instead of hoping for tips, I'm looking to make professional connections, I remind myself.

"Ah, an American. What brings you to Oxford?" He leans against the mantle of a very ornate fireplace.

I swallow the last bite of crumpet and dab at my mouth with my napkin. "International Policy and Family Studies," I tell him. "You?"

He talks about microeconomics until my eyes start to glaze, but we're soon joined by a pair of students from India, here studying the impact of colonialism, and a German dude "reading" English literature.

I lose myself in conversations about relocation, learn that the Indian folks live in my same building, and enter our campus tour buzzing. As we walk across the impressive lawn, I snap a picture to send to my mom. Then I realize it's three in the morning back home. I sigh.

———

The rest of the day is a lot of the same. I repeatedly get to say, "I'm Thora Janssen, Rhodes Fellow." I like it when people are visibly impressed by my achievements. I could get used to this, I think. But it will take some time. I have to physically restrain myself from hopping up to get everyone a tray of water glasses at lunch and I thank the staff too profusely when someone serves tea in the afternoon.

I am grateful for a lull in conversation as people sip their tea, and I take the opportunity to step back from the cluster of other international students. I stand in the window, sipping, looking out at the people milling around campus. The professors here really do wear their academic regalia, or at least they're wearing it today, billowing around campus in bright red gowns and velvet caps.

Amidst the bustle, I think I see a familiar man limping, but I convince myself it's just the jet lag. There will be no massive football players here, with or without knee rollers.

But then I hear a scraping sound, and I turn to see a man walking with a cane, entering the room and sort of dragging a cast on his right leg. He's tall and fit, with bright blue eyes and a smile that has everyone in the space walking over to greet him.

Except me. I stand with a trembling hand; not sure I can trust my eyes until he approaches, and I catch a whiff of him. Cedar and lime and, well, swagger ooze from Odin Stag. I drop my cup to the ground when I see that it's really, truly him standing here in front of me. In England. He stoops to pick up the cup with his non-cane hand. "Pretty sturdy. I'm impressed it didn't break," he says, setting the cup on the windowsill.

"What are you doing here?" All I can do is hiss at him in disbelief.

"Well, I didn't come to mop up spilled tea, that's for sure, Janssen." He leans against the wall and smirks at me like we're just joking around on campus in Pittsburgh.

"What are you *doing* here?" I repeat, crossing my arms and looking around to see if people are staring. Some are, in fact.

"I joined the crew team," he says with a shrug, and I swat him in the shoulder. He grins. "I'm serious."

I scowl and take a deep breath. "Enough, Odin. That team is for students."

He grins even bigger, flashing dimples. I realize he's wearing pants for the first time since I got to know him. He's a whole mood, in dark jeans and a nice shirt beneath a blazer that hugs his shoulder muscles. He's got a leather belt on, and my traitorous brain creates an image of him whipping it off and dropping it on the floor with a clank as he opens his pants.

"Right," he says, reminding me that I'm in public. "I also

enrolled in a sports psychology program here. Did you know they let masters students compete in sports in the UK? I'm a catch."

I blink at him, trying to understand what he's saying. That he, too, is a student. Here. Where I am a student. Close by. He leans in close and whispers. "Catch. That's a rowing joke. It slaps with the lads." And then he winks at me, and I can't take it anymore. I spin on my heel and walk out of the room.

# CHAPTER 37
# ODIN

"THORA, WAIT!" I trot after her as fast as I'm able with this walking boot. I'm making a ton of noise with this thing, but she only gets as far as the stairs before I can reach her shoulder with my palm. "Can I talk to you?"

When she turns around, I see she's crying, and she crosses her arms over her body, shivering.

"Hey." I pull her close and wrap my arms around her, letting my cane drop to the ground and not caring what happens to it. "I swear I'm not trying to be creepy."

"You followed me to another continent?"

I shrug. "Lots of places have sports psychology master's… but I was kind of limited with my options for schools that *also* have crew teams where I can compete."

"What about your foot?" She burrows her face in my shoulder and inhales, and I tuck this knowledge away that Thora likes how I smell.

"I'll be out of this boot and mostly functional by October," I explain. "I might not ever run again, but rowing is a whole different thing." I grip her shoulders and hold her a forearm's length away so I can look into her eyes. "Thora, I can compete in something. Competition has been my whole life. My whole life. I thought that was over and gone. Rowing this summer has been huge for me."

She sniffs. "I'm really happy for you then."

She bites her lip and looks off to the side and I place a finger under her chin, turning her so she faces me. "But none of it has been anywhere near as great as I feel when I'm with you, Janssen." She blinks. "You light me up. And I wanted to be close to you." I watch her inhale a shaky breath. "If you don't want me here, I'll leave. I have some options in Cardiff, and if I really have to, I can go to Stirling up in Scotland, but it'll be cold as balls, and I'd much rather be close to you. If you'll have me."

Thora doesn't say anything for a long time. She just stares at me and opens and closes her mouth. But she doesn't wriggle out of my grasp or move her hands from where she anchored them near my elbows. I take a deep breath. "And I'm sorry I was sneaky about the grant. I just really think you're awesome, and I wanted to do something nice for you but not have you feel beholden to me or something." Again, silence. "So…is it okay? That I'm here?"

"You did all that to be near me?"

I nod. Tears are really starting to flow out of her eyes now and I want to dab them away but it's my turn to feel frozen in place.

"Odin…nobody has ever done anything like this for me before."

Her confession has me beaming, and I pull her close again, putting my mouth close to her ear. "Well, Thora, nobody has ever charged up my lightning rod like you before."

She groans at the bad Norse pun, but I know I'm in now. I tip up her face again and kiss her like I've been wanting to for weeks. Ever since she ran out on me at my family's ski house. I sweep my tongue into her mouth as I pull her close and she gasps when she feels me hard against her belly.

"Odin!"

I stoop to pick up my cane and run the tip of it along her leg. "Want to get out of here?"

She tucks her hair behind her ears and nods. "My place is very close by."

I nod. "Good."

———

She holds my hand and tugs me across the lawn to a fancy-ass building worthy of my smart woman. Her flat is on the first floor, and I sigh in relief when she pulls me through the door without having to go up a single stair.

So, I use that reserved energy to shove her against the wooden door in a rush of breath and wide eyes. "I can put weight on both feet now, you know," I tell her, biting her neck. "I've been dying to fuck you against a wall."

She starts ripping open the buttons on my blazer and then pauses. "Wait. I'm mad at you."

"I'll make it up to you." I start pulling her blouse from her skirt and easing it open as she glares.

"You railroad me when you get ideas, and you don't tell me things in advance. Like with the scholarship and just... showing up here at my new school."

I pause and press a palm on the door on either side of her head. "To be fair, gorgeous, you're always telling me to shut up or go away."

She sighs at this and returns to her work ripping off my clothes. She grunts in triumph as she pulls my belt loose and drops it on the floor with a thud. I yank down her skirt and everything underneath and then nudge her legs open with my thigh, hoisting her up so she's grinding her wet little pussy on my leg. "Do you want me to go away now?"

Her eyes flash. "You fucker," she grunts, rocking her hips. "You know I want your cock."

I grin and pull it out, fisting it as she stares and licks her lips. I kick my jeans off one leg and let them dangle above my casted foot. This will have to do. "My wallet is in my pants pocket," I admit after a few seconds pinching her nipples. "But, uh, I wanted to tell you that there hasn't been anyone but you in a long time. And I just got tested for my new team…"

She looks into my eyes, nostrils flaring as she considers. "I got a physical, too. Before I came here. And there hasn't been anyone but you."

I nod. "Nobody but each other, then." I kiss her neck. "I like being yours."

"Odin. I have an IUD."

"Yeah? So, you feel safe?"

I look into her eyes and hiss as she reaches for my cock, notching it at her pussy. "I feel safe with you, Odin. I want to feel all of you."

At that, I hoist her up, and she wraps her legs around my waist. I use one hand to line myself up until she slides onto me, and I brace her against the door, grunting like a caveman as I thrust into Thora. "I'm yours," I repeat. "There's only you. Only you, Thora."

She moans and her head starts rolling around so I reach in between her legs, right above where my bare cock slides in and out of her body, feeling like magic, and I press against her clit. "I want to make you come, gorgeous. I want to make you feel good."

"Odin," she breathes and stares into my eyes. "You feel amazing." Her body starts to pulse around me. It's been a long-ass time for me, and I'm not going to last, especially not with the slick, perfect glide of her body grasping at mine like the ivy on this building.

I press harder with my thumb, swirling and chanting her name, telling her how gorgeous she looks spread open on my dick against this door, and then she screams, one wrist clamped between her lips as her heels dig into my butt.

"Thora!" Her name is a strangled burst alongside the biggest orgasm I've had in months. I lean my forehead against hers, pressing her into the door as I spurt inside her until my release is dripping out from between her legs, coating both of us.

We stare down at the mess together, panting. I ease her legs to the floor and we both sink to the rug, where I trace the pool of my sticky, white mark on her thigh.

Sweaty, filthy, exhausted, we lie in each other's arms until we're both about to fall asleep. She hums contentedly, eyes closed, dark hair tangled around my arm. "Where do you live," she asks, not moving.

"It's not far from here. Grad student housing. Or whatever they call it." I try to get comfortable, but it's no use, so I accept the hard floor meeting my hip and pull Thora close. "But I'm happy to have it sit empty if you'll let me crash here. It's a first-floor setup! No stairs." I kiss the top of her head.

"How would that work?" She rolls to her side and drapes herself across my chest, chin digging into my sternum. I like it.

I shrug. "I don't know. Same as before, I guess. You'll kick ass at school. I'll do okay at school and kick ass on the water. And if I'm lucky, you'll cheer for me in between your projects."

Thora runs a finger along my jaw and across my lips, so I kiss the wandering digit. She smiles. "That all sounds kind of nice, I guess."

# CHAPTER 38
## THORA
EARLY DECEMBER

I SHIVER on the banks of the Isis, glad Odin's mom sent me a Snuggie-type garment, even if it does have a giant stag on the back. Let the people see who I'm rooting for, I say.

While I don't understand why the Cambridge and Oxford rowing teams compete against each other in December like maniacs, I'm really happy to be here cheering for Odin. Intercollegiate rowing is different here than how sports work back in the States. Oxford has crew teams for each college within the university, but then one fancy Blue Boat team that seems to line up with infamy over here the way varsity football does in the US.

Six months ago, I would have felt guilty about taking an entire Saturday to watch someone else do things for the whole day. I would have tried to work the bar in the boat house or squeezed in some work before and after the event.

But today, I woke up in my bed with my giant boyfriend wrapped around me, had morning good-luck sex, and wandered over to the river leisurely, with a thermos of tea, to sit with the other wives and girlfriends. And I'm going to hang out for the social after the races, too.

It's been a big term for me. I say term now, like a proper

English schoolgirl, instead of semester. I've learned to relax, go sightseeing with Fern, and massage my boyfriend's shoulders after practice. He doesn't technically live with me because that would violate the rules, but we spend most of our time together.

I love it.

And I love him. I just haven't worked up the nerve to tell him yet.

I sit up straighter as I watch the judges line up the bow balls for the eight-seater boats. Odin is in the middle, a place he tells me is called the engine of the boat. He's out there in a unitard tank top, tiny socks, and little shoes that are actually built into the boat.

He's about ten weeks out of his cast now, rowing like a regular guy, he says. The official fires the starter pistol, and I hear the little shouty guys in the backs of the boats yelling at the rowers. "Power ten," they holler, and "move it."

I see them moving it, all right. I clutch my tea mug, watching Odin's shoulder muscles move in sync with the other athletes in his boat. But his body is the most beautiful. This is objective fact. Years of elite training have done him a million favors in honing his muscles.

The woman next to me elbows me. "Look at your man go!"

I nod. "He's worked really hard to be here."

The Oxford boat creeps ahead of the Cambridge boat, oars flying, and hardly any water splashes as these guys move with perfect form. I feel my cell phone buzzing in my pocket and realize Odin's mom is waiting for an update. I know they're streaming the race live online, but I'm sure there's a lag. I told Juniper I'd try to respond, but now I don't want to look away as the rival boat starts gaining on Oxford.

Yesterday afternoon, I was presenting data on the correlation between family support policies and reduced recidivism across multiple European countries' correctional systems.

Odin stood in the back, pumping his fist silently while I talked to a crowd of intellectuals from around the world. He wore a bespoke suit and then took me out to dinner at the nicest pub in town, telling me he could listen to me talk about justice and equity forever.

Old Thora would have protested and insisted on paying. When we arrived four months ago, I kept trying to give him his scholarship money back. But I've learned to appreciate the gifts he gives me as just that: no strings attached. They are offerings from his heart, things he wants me to have because it makes him happy to see me succeed.

I'm sure I would have felt proud of myself without him here. I probably would have felt confident in my role here, my power as a researcher, and knowing that my work matters. But having Odin at my side for all of it? Cheering for me and doting on me? It's like a dream I never dared to imagine.

When the coxswain notices the Cambridge boat creeping ahead and starts bellowing at Odin's team to use "Pick it up, lads!" I fly to my feet, the stag Snuggie dropping to the grass.

"Stronger strokes, Odin Stag," I scream through my cupped hands. "Eat their water!" He doesn't turn his head to face me, but I catch a glimpse of his lips turning up in a smile. The Oxford guys kick it into a new gear, and the boat catches Cambridge. I run along the course, closer to the finish rope. "Come on, Blue." My throat is hoarse as I watch the eight rowers' knees and arms moving in unison. I can see the muscles of their thighs, the ripples in their shoulders and backs as they dig and dig until it's over. As the boat glides to a stop, Odin pumps a fist in the air.

He's so happy when he's competing like his body was made to do this. Sure, he's doing great in his coursework. And he's really looking forward to working with a professional sports team someday, helping the athletes balance the mental aspects of competition … and coping with injuries that prevent them from doing what they love.

But for now, he gets another chance to be a beast. To tax his body to the limit and feel that glory from working in unison with his team.

Back on land, I see him looking for me, and I run to him, Snuggie flapping in the wind as he wraps his long, sweaty arms around me. "Thora! Did you see that shit?"

I kiss his neck, tasting salt. "I did, babe. You were amazing." He turns to wave at a passing fan, and I glance down at the thick vertical scar on his right ankle, which is a reminder that all of this is fleeting.

His muscles bulge around the spandex uniform, and his bare feet look strong, gripping the dock. He's in his element here, and he wants me to be part of it, holding me close and kissing me again and again. "Ugh," he moans. "I have to help put shit away. But you'll meet me inside?" He points at the boat house, where fans are heading, some joyful, some frustrated.

"Of course I will." My smile widens as he grips my arm. "Hey." He looks down, eyebrows raised, body poised to go and help his team with the boat. I pull his palm to my chest and press it above my ribs. "I love you, Odin. I love you so much."

The smile that splits his face is bright enough to catch a glare from the river. "Thora, I've loved you since the day you showed up in my hospital room," he says, lifting me off the ground so my face is level with his. "I've been waiting and waiting for you to feel ready to say it."

I kiss the tip of his nose. "I'm ready now," I tell him. "I never want to stop."

He kisses me, lips cold despite his internal furnace. He spins me around, and I laugh at the beauty of all of it. "I love you," I repeat.

"I love the hell out of you," he says. He sets me down. "Okay, that one was a little weird." He pulls my hand up and presses a kiss to my palm. "I love you, and I need to go put this boat away."

"Go," I tell him, and he steps backward, waving.

I snap a picture with my phone as he walks toward the boat, his torso turned toward me, arm waving, smile shooting sparks my way.

I missed a hundred messages from his family asking about the race. Apparently, the online stream didn't work. I send the photo to his family group chat, telling them, "My man, the victor. They crushed those light blue Cambridge Smurfs."

I also sent the picture to my mom, telling her I wish she could have seen Odin row, and promising her that she'll get to meet him at Christmas. Dad got a job washing dishes at the diner where Mom works, and things have been a little better back home. I might not ever be able to help lift enough stigma and baggage to help my parents directly, but I know my work will make a difference for other families like mine.

I know Odin Stag will be at my side wherever I go, rooting for me and making life work together. I used to think commitments to other people would be a burden, that opening myself up to anyone, but Fern would hold me back. I see now how these connections Odin has forced upon me have opened my world.

I grab a beer for each of us and sit on a bench at one of the long tables to wait for him.

———

My body relaxes when he arrives, gray sweats over his uniform, sandals on his still-bare feet. He slides onto the bench and pulls me into his arms, kissing me before reaching for his beer. "I love you," he says. "I'm going to say it twenty times an hour now."

"I love you too." I clink my cup against his, lean my head on his shoulder, and sip my drink happily. "Hey," I say, turning again to face him. "Did I ever thank you for following me here?"

He grins. "No, but that's okay. I can tell you need me."

"Oh, I need you, do I?"

He nods and finishes his beer in one more gulp. "You need it bad, Thora Janssen." He squints, studying me, and then leans in close. "In fact, I think we should get out of here."

"You don't want to stay and celebrate with your team?"

He shakes his head, hops to his feet, and reaches for my hand. "What I want is you, Thora. Always."

# EPILOGUE
ODIN

"MRS. JANSSEN, I couldn't eat another bite." I toss my napkin to the side and pat my stomach appreciatively. Thora was nervous as hell about coming to her parents' house for Christmas. I promised her I was absolutely fine with whatever was inside there, but her dad surprised her by revealing that he quit smoking months earlier.

Thora cried and walked through the rooms of the house, sniffing pillows and touching curtains. I mean, sure, the guy switched to nicotine gum, but it's way less stinky, and apparently, it's covered by his insurance. They have that now—insurance. Thora also cried when her parents let her help them with the paperwork for that a few months ago.

"You guys just seem so healthy," Thora sniffles. She hugs her mother tightly. They're about the same size, which is tiny. Mr. Janssen grunts and pops another piece of gum in his mouth, flicking the television over to a hockey game. I join him on the couch, looking to see my brothers on the screen. "Hey, the twins are starting," I say, and Thora pats my shoulder. She's not really a sports fan unless I'm competing, but she will agree to watch Wyatt, Wes, and Cara play soccer if I bribe her with sex. I guess I have to get her into hockey now that the Stags are back in the game.

Thora's dad stares at me like he's just putting it together that Odin Stag is related to Alder, Tucker, and Gunner Stag. "Your people play for the Fury?"

I bark out a laugh. "Well, yeah, man. Not sure about Gunny right now, actually. You know he got in a bit of trouble back in Vegas."

Thora's dad nods and crosses his arms. "Absolutely ridiculous to go there for pre-season."

I hold up my hands because what am I going to do about my brother's antics. Twenty minutes later, after a bunch of clangs from the kitchen, Thora comes up behind me again and leans her chin on my head. "You ready to go?"

I know that tone, and as much as I'd like to watch my brothers play hockey, I'd rather destroy the rental Thora and I got in my parents' neighborhood. "Thanks for everything, Mr. and Mrs. Janssen," I say, snatching Thora's coat from the banister and draping it over her shoulders. "We'll see you New Year's Eve at my uncle's house? For shrimp?"

Her parents nod and kiss her and hug her and pat my arms and then I'm back behind the driver's seat of my G Wagon, massaging the steering wheel like it's one of my girl's thighs. "Hey, lady," I whisper to the black leather glory. "You miss me?"

"Are you talking to your car? That's it, I'm not letting you anywhere near my boobs." Thora laughs and buckles her seatbelt, and I head east up Liberty Ave.

"Who said I want your crusty old boobs? Maybe I'm sick of them." It's a lie, and we both know it. I'm obsessed with Thora's bra-free rack, and I reach across to give it a pat.

I screech the car to a halt in the driveway of the rental house, and she giggles and runs up the stairs to the front door. I run right after her, still appreciating how easily I can move around in the world after six months of intense rehab.

The reward for all that is right here in front of me, stripping off her fancy pants lacy tank top, and holiday sweater.

"I love you," I tell her, tackling her to the floor inside the front door.

She pounds her fist on my chest and laughs, tugging at my own sweater. I take mercy on her and kneel above her so I can undress more easily, but I keep a knee on her leg so she can't wriggle away. I do love a game of chase with her, but she has me all worked up and I want her. Right now.

Naked, panting, I grab my length and give it a good tug while she watches, licking her lips. "You hoping for a candy cane, Thora? Something hard and sticky in your stocking?"

"You are absolutely insane." She shoots her feet around my waist and pulls me toward her body. I happily tip over and reach for her, parting her folds and finding her wet and hot and slippery.

"Oh, hello." I grin and pump a finger in and out of her body while she wriggles on the rug.

"Yes, yes, I want you, too. I'm sorry I threatened to take away my boobs. Oh, god, yes, please keep doing that." I am stroking her with two fingers now, stretching her out. I usually like to make her come at least once before I slide my cock inside her, but things are getting desperate up here for me.

With a grunt, I thrust inside my lady. "Yes, Odin, god, yes," she says, nails poking into the tattoos on my shoulder blades. She sinks her teeth into the side of my neck, and I growl, pulling back onto my knees and hauling her ass off the ground so her hips are on my lap.

I'm very deep inside her this way, and I can watch her chest shaking as we slam together. "This is all yours, Thora." I punctuate each word with another thrust. "Every. Thing. I. Have."

"Love you," she wails, bringing her hand between her legs.

"Yes, beautiful, touch yourself for me." I wrap an arm under each of her thighs, spreading her even wider and giving me more leverage to pull her into my body.

Thora releases strangled sounds of ecstasy as her fingers fly over her clit, her other hand scrambling to grab my arm, my leg, the rug. I feel it when she starts to come, and I soar over the cliff alongside her, grunting with the effort and then flopping forward to join her on the rug.

"Merry Christmas," she whispers, eyes fluttering open like she can't decide if she can remain awake.

"Hm," is all I can manage in return.

"We hardly ever do it in a bed," she says, rolling onto her back and blowing hair out of her mouth. "Why is that?"

"Because we have imagination. Because I can't control myself when I'm near you. Because the whole world is a canvas for our art."

I roll onto my back and lace my fingers together behind my head.

Thora roars with laughter and sits up. "Odin Stag, the things that fall out of your mouth."

"You love it," I say, winking at her in the glow of the twinkle lights on our rented mantle.

She sighs and lies back down, arms around my middle, head on my chest. "Yeah," she says. "I really do."

*Thank you for reading Forging Chaos! If you want to know what trouble Gunnar Stag gets into, read his book*
*Playing for Keeps.*

*Can't get enough of Odin and Thora? My newsletter subscribers get a bonus scene.*
*Sign up at LaineyDavis.com or scan the QR code.*

Since You've Bean Gone (Ethan and Lia) *part of the Farm 2 Forking series

*Binge the following series in eBook, paperback, or audio!*

**Brady Family Series**

Foundation: A Grouchy Geek Romance (Zack and Nicole)

Suspension: An Opposites Attract Romance (Liam and Maddie)

Inspection: A Silver Fox Romance (Kellen and Elizabeth)

Vibration: An Accidental Roommates Romance (Cal and Logan)

Current: A Secret Baby Romance (Orla and Walt)

Restoration: A Silver Fox Redemption Romance (Mick and Celeste)

**Oak Creek Series**

The Nerd and the Neighbor (Hunter and Abigail)

The Botanist and the Billionaire (Diana and Asa)

The Midwife and the Money (Archer and Opal)

The Planner and the Player (Fletcher and Thistle)

**Stone Creek University**

Deep in the Pocket: A Football Romance

Hard Edge: A Hockey Romance

Possession: A Football Romance